I MARRIED A NAGA

Prime Mating Agency

REGINE ABEL

COVER DESIGN BY
Regine Abel

CHARACTER ART BY
Sam Griffin

This book uses mature language and explicit sexual content. It is not intended for anyone under the age of 18.

This book is a work of fiction. Names, characters, places, and incidents are either products of the author's imagination or are used fictitiously. Any resemblance to actual persons, living or dead, events, or locales is entirely coincidental.

CONTENTS

I MARRIED A NAGA

She got more than she bargained for.

When Serena comes to Trangor to participate in the First Hunt, the last thing she expects is to find herself forced to marry an Ordosian… or be executed. She knows nothing of his people, nothing of him, except that he's got fangs, scales, and a crazy long tail. Serena only has to play the part of being a wife for six months, and then she'll be free to leave. But Szaro seems to have other plans. He's big, intimidating, and definitely not human. Yet, how can she remain indifferent when he does everything to please her?

From the moment he lays eyes on Serena, Szaro is fascinated by the delicate human female. Deceptively fragile in appearance, she's a fearless and skilled hunter. The lingering taste of her scent on his tongue is intoxicating. Claiming her to save her life is no hardship for him. Overcoming their differences and convincing her to stay willingly is a challenge he relishes. But will that prove more than either of them can handle?

DEDICATION

To anyone who had the courage to do the right thing, even at a high cost to themselves. Sooner or later, and usually when you least expect it, Karma will have your back.

CHAPTER 1
SERENA

Shifting restlessly on my feet, I glanced at my First Hunt rivals as we waited to board the transport shuttles. All the big names had come out to play. No wonder, considering the more-than-generous prizes on the line. While a badass hunter myself, I held no illusions I could win the grand prize. At five million credits, that purse verged on the obscene. However, unlike most other hunts, this one guaranteed everyone would come out a winner based on their performance. Therefore, participation had been by-invitation-only, sent out to well-established hunters with the Galactic Hunters Federation.

Twenty shuttles filled the massive hangar of the Federation's base camp—one of the few non-native buildings on Trangor. None of us had ever set foot on this 'primitive' planet. Until recently, we'd all believed it to be a savage world, solely populated by wild beasts. But just like Earth, a single sentient species dominated the food chain—snake-like people called the Ordosians. We didn't know much about them. They didn't care to mingle with off-worlders and especially didn't want us traipsing around their world. That the Federation had managed to secure their permission to hold this hunt was a miracle.

A chime resonated in the large hall, silencing the chatter among the hunters. Bron Kflen, the Federation Master Hunter, stood on a small pedestal to address us one last time before boarding. The Edocit male—a dryad species—had been a legend in his prime.

"Hunters, welcome to the First Hunt of Trangor," Bron said in a booming voice. "You are here because you are the best of the best. We want an efficient hunt, with clean, merciful kills, and as little damage as possible to your targets' organs as they are to be used for vital medical research. Therefore, on top of the flat fee for each kill, we will award a credit bonus for clean kills, earning you additional points to win the grand prize. So, make sure to claim your kills with the beacons provided so our extraction teams can recover them swiftly."

An excited buzz coursed through the crowd. These types of hunts were few and far between. While some hunters swam in credits up to their eyeballs, others barely made enough to make a living, maintain and upgrade their gear, and pay the entrance fee of most of the general events. This would provide a good padding for those with shallow pockets. I didn't come even close to qualifying as rich, but I didn't struggle to make ends meet. This would beef up my comfortable nest egg.

"We have loaded your speeders or gliders into the shuttles that will take you to the sector you have selected to hunt," Bron continued. "Remember that you are to *exclusively* hunt Flayers. *Nothing else!* The Ordosian only allowed this to control their population."

Apparently, those creatures reproduced at a ridiculously high rate. Every year, during the birthing season, any adult Flayer that was unmated, sick, or old was cast out of their territory to make room for the newborns. Those outcasts would rampage through the land, wreaking havoc among the vulnerable species they encountered. Our job was to eradicate that roaming threat.

"Before your departure, please check again that your map has been properly synced and that it clearly displays the authorized hunting areas. Do NOT, I repeat, DO NOT trespass outside the authorized boundaries. The Ordosians consider those other areas as holy grounds. They *will* execute you if you are caught in the forbidden areas."

Like me, most of the nearly 100 hunters in the room double-checked that the map integrated in our bracers functioned properly.

"A tracker will warn you if you get too close to the border, and even more so if you cross it. Should that happen, turn back immediately, and pray you weren't seen," Bron said sternly. "If you are caught trespassing or gratuitously harming the local fauna or flora, we will not lift a finger if the Ordosians retaliate. It has taken us a long time to secure this event with the locals. See that you don't ruin it for everyone. And play nicely with each other. If any of you are caught deliberately endangering your competitors, be it by luring or any other underhanded method, you will be banned and forfeit whatever earnings you might have acquired."

A smirk stretched my lips as a few hunters cringed. In this highly competitive world, some showed few scruples when it came to getting the upper hand.

"But enough with the speeches and warnings. In a few seconds, the number of your shuttle will be communicated to your bracer. Good luck, and good hunt!" Bron concluded.

Enthusiastic cheers rose throughout the room, accompanied by discreet notification sounds as everyone received their number. Lucky number thirteen for me. I picked up my backpack sitting on the floor at my feet, shouldered it, and made my way to my assigned transport along with four males. Although only a fifth of the hunters in attendance were female, our numbers were steadily increasing every season.

My heart sank upon recognizing a familiar face boarding ahead of me. Baron—real name Bayrohnziyiek—was a bonafide asshole. Of course, the Zamorian male had to head in the same sector I had chosen. He was as tall and massive as he was brutal and ruthless, not to mention prone to cheating and hurting his rivals. Like all the people of his species, he vaguely resembled a grey-skinned orc with four arms, four eyes, and a long, straight mane held in a single braid. I couldn't believe he'd been invited to an event that sought to be clean and ethical. Apparently, his high hunter ranking had convinced the selection committee to turn a blind eye.

I needed to steer clear of that jerk. Anyway, he would be gunning for the biggest prey: mature male Flayers. They were harder to kill but worth more credits and points. I'd set my focus on the medium-sized ones. I could kill them faster and with less risk of serious injury. For me, this hunt wasn't about trying to strike it rich. I only wanted to pad my bank account, take part in this unique experience against a brand-new beast, and explore a world on which few people could boast of having ever set foot.

As soon as we settled into the passenger seats of the shuttle, it took off heading northeast. The broad windows gave me my first breathtaking view of Trangor. The clear blue sky had a light greenish tinge to it. Below, dense forests made of strange, prehistoric-looking trees, spread as far as the eye could see. Some vaguely resembled dragon trees, others monkey puzzle trees, and others could have been baobabs whose trunks had been carefully wrapped in braided bark.

After a relatively brief journey, the shuttle landed in a vast clearing. Based on the scanner readings provided by the Federation, while this area had some good pockets of rampaging Flayers, their numbers wouldn't be too overwhelming for a single human hunter. Most of my rivals had headed southwest and northwest where throngs of beasts were swarming. I had expected Baron to go that route for a chance at more kills.

After wishing good luck to my *competition*, I took my speeder out of the hold and double-checked that my few survival supplies were still securely stashed in the storage space under my seat. Giddy with excitement, I took off, heading north, while the others scattered in a different direction. Firing up my long-range scanner, I went on the prowl.

To my delight, it took less than ten minutes for the first dots to appear on my scanner revealing nearby Flayers. I made a beeline for one that seemed to be somewhat isolated from the others. Lucky for me, although decent-sized, the beast wasn't one of the massive mature males that could tear you to shreds before you had time to blink. It would be a good warmup before I started gunning for more challenging prey.

Flayers were truly ugly beasts. The lower half of their bodies look like that of a short centipede with only four legs on each side. Attached to it was a long torso that could have belonged to a chubby human. It possessed a pair of insect-like limbs with scythe-like appendages that could slice a person in half in a single swipe. Its neck, almost a meter long, ended in a round head that was one huge mouth filled with dagger teeth. All around that mouth and along the sides of its neck were at least two dozen eyes that gave it a 360-degree view of its surroundings.

Thankfully, it had poor hearing, and its vision had a fairly short range. However, it was very sensitive to vibrations on the ground and in the air around it. I stopped my speeder at a safe enough distance from the beast and activated my stealth shield. Facing off against one of these creatures would be suicidal. Not only were they extremely fast, but once they had you in their sights, they became relentless until you sat inside their bellies. And right now, my target was on the prowl for something to snack on.

Aside from the Flayer's occasional rattling growl and the wind whistling in the leaves, the eerie silence surrounding us confirmed the rest of the fauna—even the birds—had taken cover during the stampede. Granted, it was far from a stampede in this area, which was why I'd chosen it. But out west, large herds of Flayers were rampaging through the region, devouring everything in their path like a swarm of locust. Apparently, this occurred once a year on Trangor, hence the need to thin the herd to keep them from exterminating weaker species.

The trick was to basically knock them off their feet. Then they became as helpless as a turtle on its back. Lucky for me, the wind blew northeast, driving my scent away from my quarry. What they lacked in sight and hearing, Flayers made up for with the sensitivity of their noses. I removed my crossbow and loaded it with bolts. The state-of-the-art weapon with aim assist allowed me to pre-lock the targets, a very tiny spot below the protective scale that covered the knees of its front legs. Once I fired, I would have a very small window in which to perform a clean kill. Failing that, things could get messier.

Heart pounding, adrenaline pumping through my veins, I quietly closed the distance with my prey. Stopping a little over ten meters away, I took in a deep breath, focused, then let my bolts fly. Even as they shot forward within a split second from each other, I took aim at the creature's face, blocking everything around me but my target. Time seemed to slow as my bolts found their marks, burying themselves in the soft tissue below the knee shells of the Flayer. Its two front legs folded, and the beast pitched forward. While its torso bowed down, it stretched its neck forward to shriek, opening wide its tooth-filled maw.

In the critical few seconds I had to react, I zoomed in and aimed at the spot right above the purple protrusion at the back of its throat—the equivalent of a human's uvula—and fired. I cursed under my breath even as the bolt left my crossbolt, knowing I had missed the shot when the creature tilted its head to the side. Without blinking, I adjusted and fired again, breaking into a run even as my arrow left my weapon. The loud cracking sound that reached me as I rushed the beast confirmed my second shot had hit its mark.

I shouted in victory while the creature's upper body thrashed on the ground and its back legs scrambled backwards in a blind attempt to flee the source of pain. Without slowing down from my run, I jumped onto the creature's back while drawing my dagger. Sitting on its long neck, feeling like a cowgirl in a rodeo as it tried to buck me off in its agony, I grabbed the end of my bolt protruding through the back of its skull where it had breached its unique weak spot. Lifting it up, I stabbed my dagger downward, severing its spine and all blood flow to the brain. A violent tremor shook the creature, and then it went still.

I pulled out the dagger and hopped off the creature. Wasting no time, I retrieved my beacon gun and shot a single disc in the opening at the back of the Flayer's skull. A bluish shimmer spread around the beast as the beacon began to pulsate with a faint, luminous glow. On top of confirming this as my kill for both score and payment, the beacon sent a signal to the extraction team. Furthermore, the shimmering dome it created kept the kill in a form of stasis so the organs wouldn't spoil before recovery. It also acted as a repellent against any roaming wildlife that thought to enjoy a free meal.

Stoked by this promising start, I cleaned my dagger and returned to my speeder to search for my next prey. For the next few hours, I continued my efforts, exterminating a far greater number of beasts than I had expected. Granted, I faced a few close calls, but what was a hunt without some hair-raising moments?

As the sun lowered on the horizon, I decided to camp instead of returning to the base. I was far too deep in the north to justify that trip back. With the Saroyan mountains a short distance from here, I would likely find a cave or some sort of overhang that would provide a half decent shelter for the night. I decided to move northeast, closer to the Ordosian territories. They would be safer with a lot fewer roaming creatures as the locals would be steadfast in clearing them.

Sure enough, I found a nice little natural cave in the middle of nowhere. Still, I placed a series of motion detectors in a wide radius around the cave in case something came lurking while I slept. I retrieved the inflatable mattress from my speeder. While I could rough it out with the best of them, I enjoyed my creature comforts whenever possible. This clever design allowed the mattress to compact into what resembled a thick book. But when unfolded, it inflated to a twin-size mattress. It wasn't fancy, but it sure beat sleeping on hard stones and rocks.

I settled for eating some of my energy bars and washed them down with some water. As was my wont when on the trail, I rarely bothered with proper meals. Lighting a fire and cooking a catch had a way of attracting the wrong kind of attention. Once the hunt was over though, I would pamper myself with a five-star meal in a luxurious restaurant on my way home. As I settled for the night, I pulled up the scoring results for today's round on my datapad. To my surprise, I had ranked 22nd, much higher than I had expected considering the caliber of my rivals.

My jaw dropped when I saw Baron not only in first place, but incredibly far ahead of everyone else. There was no way a single person could have achieved such a score by themselves. And yet, there was no way to cheat. You could only score by tagging a kill. How the heck was he killing so many mature male Flayers, so damn fast? I didn't doubt for a minute that he had found a way to game the system. It just pissed me off that he would win the grand prize when I knew in my gut that he did not deserve it.

Shrugging it off, I turned in for the night.

CHAPTER 2
SERENA

Morning came quickly. Although I could have slept for a couple more hours, I decided to make an early start. By my calculations, I'd earned between 25,000 and 35,000 credits on my first day. I wanted to match, and maybe even surpass, that score today. I came here hoping to make 50,000 to 70,000 credits through the entirety of the event. But at this current pace, I could potentially double that. What a fine haul that would be!

As soon as I got on my speeder, I fired up my wide-range scanner, thinking to head west while remaining up north. That plan changed really quickly when, to my surprise, a large number of Flayers popped up on my scanner. They appeared to be spread alongside the border of the Ordosian territory, a short distance north from here. They were spread out enough that I would be able to take them on, as long as I maintained the element of surprise. With stealth, those badass beasts were a breeze to kill. But once you lost that element of surprise, your chances of survival dropped by half.

I made haste towards the location of the first creature. To my dismay, it was a wide open plain, a short distance from the woods that marked the beginning of the forbidden territory. This could seriously complicate things if a bunch of Flayers were clustered together. But as I closed the distance with my quarry, my jaw all but dropped at the spectacle that awaited me.

A massive Flayer lay on its side, dead, unmarked, and with not a single soul in sight to claim it. I glanced around but found no one in the immediate vicinity. Not believing my luck, I approached carefully with my stealth shield still activated. I stopped next to it, still not detecting anyone nearby. I ran a quick scan over the creature, confirming the death was recent. I didn't know how much damage the organs had sustained by now, but it was still worth a nice chunk of credits. I disembarked my speeder and crouched in front of the beast. The kill had been phenomenal. No visible marks of any other wounds but a single stab right beneath the jugular and straight through the spine. This shit was worth maximum points—assuming the decay had not been too advanced.

Without further hesitation, I grabbed my beacon gun and claimed the beast.

I hopped back on my speeder and raced to the next Flayer indicated on my scanner. The same heavenly present awaited me. I deduced then that the Ordosians had been taking out the creatures roaming a little too close to their territory, leaving the bounty for yours truly to claim. And claim I did. Sadly, I had to pass on the fifth one I saw as the wretched creature had keeled over only a couple of meters inside the Ordosian territory. Although I couldn't see any of the locals nearby, my ass wasn't taking any chances over greed. By the time I reached the eighth kill, a sense of unease began to seep in. Those were extremely recent kills. But there shouldn't be this many mature—almost elder—Flayers in this area. Where the fuck were they all coming from?

As I leaned down to claim the beast, the sudden impression of being observed made me snap my head up. It took me a moment before I spotted the being observing me. My blood froze in my veins, and I reined in the instinctive panic that wanted to settle in when I recognized the imposing silhouette of an Ordosian by the tree line. Although I knew myself to still be in the authorized hunting grounds, I double checked my bracer to make sure I hadn't broken their rule. My bracer had been steadily pulsating around my wrist as a warning that I was getting a little too close for comfort to the forbidden territories.

I looked back at the Ordosian, only to see two more had joined him. Just when I was about to freak out, the first one—who appeared to be their leader—gestured for the others to follow as they continued their way north, ignoring me. Their demeanor had not been threatening in any way, but it still made me wonder if maybe I should cut and run.

Technically, unclaimed dead Flayers are fair game.

Indeed, I wasn't breaking any rules. If they wanted me to piss off, I didn't doubt for a minute they would say as much. In my usual too-bold-for-my-own-good way, I decided to push on. I found and claimed three more dead Flayers before I finally came up on the warriors that had been making me rich this morning. There were six of them, the three I had encountered earlier among them. Fascinated, I remained at a safe distance to watch them battle the creature. Sadly, it had followed them inside the forbidden territory, beyond reach of my greedy claim.

To my surprise, their method couldn't have been more different than what I had expected. I'd been so certain that, in order to achieve such clean kills, they'd been using some sort of stun gun or other means of paralysis. Instead, the Ordosians came at it with pretty much their bare hands, but especially with their tails. I had seen pictures of the Naga-like beings. With their upper bodies remarkably human—aside from their facial features and the king cobra hood around their heads—and their lower bodies consisting in the tail of a snake, they were a wonder to behold.

From where I stood, they appeared to 'stand' two meters tall, and their winding tail behind them measured at least another three meters. Two of the Ordosians essentially acted as bait, each one trying to lure the Flayer in a different direction, almost paralyzing it with confusion. The other four, shifting the color of their scales into a fairly effective camouflage, threw themselves at the beast, two on each side. Or so I thought. Instead of catching its legs with their hands—as I first believed they were crazily trying to do—they used their palms on the ground as pivots then whipped their tail at their prey's legs. Not only did they knock them from under the creature, but they each held on to two legs by wrapping their tail around them.

Helplessly splayed on the ground, the beast reared its head and tried to use its long neck to snap at one of Ordosians pinning it down. But one of the two males that had been luring it—the one I presumed to be their leader—turned back and caught the Flayer's head, wrapping his muscular arm right below its jaw and his tail around the neck before squeezing. Effectively immobilized, the beast never saw the blade their leader stabbed into the vulnerable spot right below its jugular until it reached the back of the throat. He then tilted the dagger upward to slip through the small crease of the protective bone to sever the spine. The creature shuddered then went still.

Another flawless kill.

It had taken them barely a minute from start to finish to take down the beast, their movements perfectly coordinated. The jugular kill was the best for anyone strong enough to take the creature head on. Unfortunately, I couldn't do that with my bolts —they would simply hit the protective bone and not sever the spine. First, you needed to stab at a 30-degrees angle upward, then tilt down at a 45-degree angle downward.

But no sooner did they release the dead creature than their collective heads snapped towards me, their forked lizard tongues flicking in my direction. My blood froze, realizing they either smelled or sensed my presence. We'd been warned that stealth technology wouldn't fool Ordosians, although they hadn't gone into detail as to how exactly that species bypassed our camouflage.

I hesitated for a second, debating if I should hightail it or reveal myself. In the end, I chose to reveal myself and deactivated my stealth shield. There was nothing wrong with watching, and fleeing could imply nefarious intent. Swallowing hard, I moved a little closer, although remaining at a safe enough distance from them and their boundary. The way they all simultaneously tilted their heads to the side as they examined me might have been creepy had their faces shown any type of aggression. Instead, they evinced only curiosity.

They're not the blood-thirsty savages the Federation has been hinting at.

Then again, I couldn't blame the Federation for depicting them as hostile to keep us from messing with the locals and causing unnecessary diplomatic incidents.

"Fantastic teamwork," I shouted in Universal. "I'm impressed."

From their reaction, I believed they'd just snorted. I grinned sheepishly, a bit stunned by my own ballsy behavior. Four of them started north. The leader and another Ordosian stayed behind. I bowed my head in goodbye, intent on resuming my journey alongside their border to see if my lucky streak had ended. But before I could even advance by a few meters, their leader called out to me.

"Human!" he shouted, his voice powerful, with a slight throaty rattling that gave it a badass edge as well as being sexy as fuck.

I stopped and cast a curious look at him. My jaw dropped when, instead of responding, he and the other male by his side each grabbed a front leg of the Flayer and dragged him towards me, outside of the restricted zone.

"No way…" I whispered to myself.

I flew my speeder close to them, stopping a couple of meters away before disembarking. Those Ordosians were truly impressive in the flesh. With my height of 6'1, I usually didn't feel too scrawny around other species. But these guys, especially the one I presumed to be the hunt leader, made me feel like a delicate little flower. From where his tail touched the ground to the top of the hood on his head, he towered over me by at least a foot. His broad shoulders, bulging biceps, and insanely cut abs would have had most human males dying with envy.

And every hot-blooded woman wetting her panties.

Okay, the snake tail, the forked tongue, the slit nostrils, and the lizard eyes were a little freaky, but that hood on his head was badass. He had some pretty damn sexy and incredibly human-looking lips. If he'd had legs instead of that tail, I would have been attracted to him.

"Thank you," I said, feeling a bit intimidated.

His tongue flicked in my direction. That unnerved the heck out of me and somewhat crashed his hotness level. What information was he gathering about me with his tongue? We knew far too little about their species. Whatever it told him, he seemed amused, and a barely-there smirk stretched his plush lips. That annoyed me for some reason.

Without a word, he lifted the head of the Flayer, turning it to the side in order to expose the wound in its neck. He slithered back, allowing me to shoot my beacon in the opening to claim the beast. The shimmering stasis dome appeared over the Flayer, and I took a step back before looking up at the Ordosian.

"Well, thanks again. That's very generous of you," I said with a nervous laughter, feeling utterly awkward for a reason I couldn't explain.

He flicked his tongue a couple more times at me, the narrow slit of his pale green eyes widening slightly as he stared intently at me.

"Stay safe, human," he finally said, before turning and slithering away with his companion.

I remained transfixed, watching the sensual swaying of their hips—well, his hips mainly—as they moved at dizzying speed, no doubt to catch up to the rest of their party. The movement more or less reminded me of those of a merengue or Latin dancer.

Yep, pretty hot other than the snake parts.

I got back on my speeder to seek my next target only to finally get the answer to the mystery behind my abnormal good luck. Just as I stopped next to the new dead beast, I looked in the distance for the other Flayer my scanner was picking up. To my shock, about 300 meters ahead, I spotted Baron luring the massive creature. He fired something in the direction of the Ordosian forbidden territory before going into stealth mode. The beast continued towards the Zamorian's projectile. As soon as it reached it, it stomped around that location and rubbed its face on the ground.

Some sort of pheromone... The bastard! He's luring them for the Ordosians to kill.

And he was likely moving here to come claim this beast. On instinct, I jumped off of my speeder, deactivated my stealth shield, and whipped out my beacon gun to mark the beast.

"HEY! This is MY kill!" the Zamorian shouted, coming out of stealth as his speeder raced towards me.

Holding his gaze unwaveringly, I made a show of activating my body cam, ensuring it captured him still approaching on his speeder as I shot my beacon into the creature. In the distance, the Flayer he had lured continued to mess with whatever scent had enthralled it.

"You fucking thief!" he roared, jumping off of his speeder before it had fully stopped to come towering over me.

"Control yourself, Bayrohnziyiek," I hissed in his face, taking on a bold and cocky stance, despite my heart trying to pound its way out of my chest. That beastly alien could grab each of my limbs with his four arms and rip me apart without breaking a sweat. "You don't want to do anything you might regret," I added, pointing at the body cam on my shoulder.

He fisted his four hands and bared his sharp teeth at me, the tusks framing them appearing to grow even bigger in his anger. In that instant, I knew beyond the shadow of a doubt that he probably would have killed or maimed me without this blessed protection provided by the Federation. Once activated, the camera immediately sent live footage—both audio and video—directly to the Federation base camp. It helped in getting to the truth of any conflict, and often avoiding 'unfortunate' incidents. When big money prizes were on the line, in the heat of the hunt and with adrenaline pumping through their veins, people's baser instincts easily clouded their moral compass.

"You stole from me, you *kahbra*!" he shouted.

"How can I steal a kill that you didn't make and were nowhere near when I claimed it?" I asked. "Or the dozen or so that I claimed along the way here?"

His four eyes widened, their orange color turning a dark red as his head jerked up to look above my head, as if he could see the dead beasts I'd claimed in the distance. As dangerous as it was for me to further provoke his anger, I needed to out him and get things on the record now, with his reaction to my accusations.

"As per the rules, a dead Flayer is fair-game—first come, first serve. But who would have thought so many Flayers would roam this area that was deemed the safest?" I continued with fake astonishment. "Surely, no hunter would *dare* use pheromones to lure the beasts here so that the locals can do all the work for them and then reap the reward. That would not only be cheating, it would also be grossly unethical, and could cause a diplomatic nightmare with the Ordosians for endangering their people."

The Zamorian's face closed off. "I have witnessed no such behavior," he ground out between his teeth.

"I'm sure you haven't," I replied in a syrupy sweet voice. "But I do wonder what is causing that Flayer over there to be so fascinated with the ground," I added, leaning to the side so that my camera could capture the beast in the distance. "You'd think it stumbled on its version of catnip."

"Maybe it did," Baron snapped.

"Maybe. I guess we'll never know," I replied, matter-of-factly, before my tone and expression hardened. "But as much as I enjoy this little chat, I need to get back to the hunt. We've been brought here to help thin the herd of Flayers. Should they mysteriously continue to threaten the safety of the Ordosians at their border, I dare hope the Federation will take radical measures to eradicate the problem. Good hunting to you."

Without waiting for his response, I got back on my speeder. Movement at the edge of my vision startled me. To my dismay, I noticed a few of the Ordosians warriors I'd seen earlier standing by the forest, looking at us. Fuck me sideways! I hoped to God they didn't think me in on it with that idiot. Glaring at Baron, I took off. After turning off my body cam, I activated my stealth shield and continued the journey north.

I didn't expect to find any other unclaimed dead Flayers. In truth, even if I did, I doubted I would have wanted to claim them anymore. What had initially been my 'lucky' streak now left a bad taste in my mouth. Were the Ordosians aware that Baron had been using them as grunts for easy points? Were they pissed?

The ones I'd met hadn't seemed angry… at least not with me.

This could still cause a really bad diplomatic conflict that could make the locals kick us off their planet. I wasn't ready to leave. I wanted to get the job done and then take a few days to explore all the authorized areas of this gorgeous world before the departure of the last transport ship off of this rock.

For now, I wanted to get to the Bayagi River, refill my water bottles, and have a quick lunch. Then, I would head west where more scattered clusters of Flayers had been reported. My anger flared again as I flew past far too many claimed dead beasts and spotted a few more living ones wandering near the border. I stopped to kill a couple along the way but didn't stick around to claim the ones the Ordosian patrols were already engaging.

However, as I closed the distance with the river, it wasn't its mesmerizing aqua color that held my attention, but the two large Flayers getting dangerously close to the Ordosian border. For the past ten minutes, I hadn't seen a single dead beast or Ordosian patrol. Even if I wanted to take them out, I would have a hard time surviving two at once. I could only presume the wind had blown the pheromones this far north. The real problem was that my scanner was also picking up a heck of a lot of lifeforms nearby, in and around the river within the Ordosian territory. Were they animals or…?

I never got to finish that thought. One of the Flayers roared, his companion echoing him seconds later, and then countless voices in the distance responded with panicked screams. By their high pitch, it didn't sound like the warriors I had encountered earlier, but their females. I reached the edge of the Ordosian territory only to see the beasts charging deeper into the forest in the direction of the dots scattering on my scanner. My stomach knotted painfully as I sat on my speeder, still camouflaged, fighting the urge to go assist them.

Surely, they have some warriors with them to handle the beasts, right?

But my brain froze at the sound of a high-pitched voice calling out a name, and then an older voice calling out another. Time appeared to slow as one of the Flayers switched direction to chase after a four-legged, smaller creature that charged it before veering off, away from the fleeing females.

A pet, trying to protect its masters.

Behind it, a young Ordosian, maybe five or six-year-old, was chasing after it while his mother—I presumed—shouted for him to come back. I turned on my body cam, already knowing what I would do. The Flayer swiped its scythe-like arm, striking the rump of the pet with the back of its 'hand.' The force of the blow sent the poor creature flying a short distance before it smashed against the thick trunk of a tree. From this distance, I couldn't hear what sound it made, but the way it flopped to the ground and remained still indicated it had either been killed or sustained some serious injuries.

Both Flayers turned their attention to the child. They charged the little Ordosian, who finally realized what danger his concern for his pet had put him in. He shouted in fear, turning back towards his mother, who was also dashing towards him.

I didn't hesitate.

The previous vibration of my bracer—warning me of my much too close proximity with the Ordosian border—went into overdrive, and an alarm sound went off as soon as I crossed it. I silenced it.

Racing forward, I reached for one of the three bolas hanging below my weapons pouch under my speeder's handle for easy access. As I would never get into throwing range of the beasts before they caught their prey, I blew my horn, emitting a painfully strident sound that bothered even me. The Flayers jerked their long necks around to look behind for the source of the noise. While the eyes along their necks granted them a 360-degree view, the ones on their forehead had a better 'long-range' vision. However, as I was still in stealth mode, they saw nothing.

Still, that slowed them down a little, giving me a chance to make up some ground as they turned back to focus on their quarry. I spun the bola above my head, taking aim at the biggest of the two beasts before letting it fly. For the creatures, the weapon would have appeared to have come out of thin air. The bola found its mark, wrapping around two of the Flayer's back legs, making it stumble and fall.

It cried out, first in surprise, second in agony as the weapon —set to lethal instead of capture—began to tighten, the nanites of the cable reshaping it to sharp edges that cut through scales, flesh and bones. With his prey almost within range, the other Flayer didn't stop to look at its injured companion. But I already had another bola spinning just for it.

With less than ten meters between them and the beast, the mother reached her son and picked him up. At the same time, the second bola worked its magic, knocking the Flayer flat on its belly. The female appeared to freeze in terror as, carried by its momentum, it slid on the ground over a few more meters towards her.

"RUN!" I shouted to the female in Universal. Her head jerked up, and I realized she couldn't see me. I deactivated my stealth shield. "GO! RUN AWAY!"

Her eyes widened as she saw me, hand raised, holding a grenade, rounding up at high speed near the first Flayer that was already scrambling back up on its remaining legs. She turned around and dashed away, her speed slightly impeded by the weight of her child, but still moving much faster than the child on his own would have managed.

I threw the flash grenade on the ground, right in front of the first beast, blinding it. It screeched in pain, shaking its head, completely disoriented. Circling back, I zipped past the second Flayer, also getting back on its remaining legs. I blared my horn to get its attention and picked up my last bola and flung it at the still-roaring, blinded beast. It easily wrapped around its neck, and immediately went to work, sawing right through it. The Flayer fell to the ground, thrashing, while the wire of the bola slowly beheaded it. My stomach churned. This was not the way of the Hunter. You made a quick, clean, as-painless-as-possible kill. But this was survival.

Despite its two missing legs, the remaining Flayer was quickly gaining on me. I barely managed to avoid the lethal swipe of its scythed limb before throwing a flash grenade in front of it. Circling back around, navigation made more challenging by the thick trees surrounding us, I grabbed the crossbow hanging on my back. I took aim, blocking out the deafening sound of the beast's shrieks. His screams choked when my bolt perfectly struck the vulnerable spot under its uvula. It flopped to the ground. I jumped off my speeder and ran towards it to grant it a swift death.

While this had been a much cleaner kill than the first one, I had no intentions of claiming either. Heart pounding, I ran back to my speeder. But now that the growling and screeching of the beasts had gone silent, the sound of hooves pounding the ground resonated loudly above the blood roaring in my ears. I'd no sooner begun speeding away than my bracer blinked, indicating a dozen quickly approaching dots.

My blood turned to ice as I spotted the first silhouettes of Ordosians riding on top of Drayshans. Those mounts were insanely fast. For a split second, I considered going into stealth and making a run for it. However, even if I managed to outrun them, the Ordosians had previously seen my face, my scent was all over the place, and if they confronted the Federation about the trespasser, Master Hunter Bron would be forced to give me away.

I saved two of theirs. Surely, that will justify my trespass.

Reining in the fear twisting my insides, I stopped my speeder, turned around, and waited for the dozen Ordosians to surround me. Their faces held none of the previous curiosity. All of their eyes containing nothing but a murderous glimmer.

CHAPTER 3
SZARO

Rage boiled in my guts. We'd allowed the off-worlders onto Trangor to lessen the burden on us controlling the Flayer rampage during birthing season. Instead, they had brought greater danger to our doorstep. Despite the Zamorian's shameless tactics to make us kill the beasts on his behalf, he'd had the good sense of staying outside of our hallowed grounds. After the intriguing little human had confronted him about it, he had left.

Or so we thought.

As soon as the proximity detectors went off, confirming an off-worlder had trespassed, we jumped onto our Drayshans to go confront the perpetrator. I couldn't wait to get my hands on him. I would take great pleasure in hearing his bones being crushed beneath my tail.

To my shock, as we closed in on the trespasser's location—far too close to where our females were teaching our young to swim—a familiar delicate scent, laced with fear, settled on my tongue.

It can't be...

And yet, there she was, sitting on her speeder. Nearby, the savaged corpses of two Flayers. My brain froze with horror at the thought of executing a female… *this* female. Why did she do this? Why would she trespass when she'd been so respectful throughout the day?

But even as we closed the distance with her, the sight of Mandha and five other hunters racing towards our location took me aback.

What are they doing here?

"Intruder!" Raskier shouted, as his Drayshan barreled down on the female.

"Wait! It's not what you think!" the female shouted back in Universal. She dismounted from her speeder and raised her palms, head bowed, in what I assumed to be a submissive stance. "Your females were being attacked! I came to help!"

My heart leapt upon hearing her words. Yes, our females and offspring had been nearby. Based on her earlier behavior, it would make sense for this to have been the reason for her trespass.

But she has trespassed, nonetheless. The rules are clear.

We stopped our mounts near her. Between my Hunters and Mandha's, the female found herself completely surrounded. I unwrapped my tail from my Drayshan's hind horn, and slipped down the recess on its back, the others imitating me. The female swallowed hard and stared at us, wide-eyed, as we moved in. I hated the scent of her fear.

"I swear, I only came here to protect your people. This wasn't for the hunt," the female continued with a somewhat trembling voice. "I didn't even claim them! That mother and her child wouldn't have made it. Those two Flayers killed their pet, sent him crashing against a tree over there," she added, pointing to the northwest. "And then they started chasing after the little one. So yes, I broke the rule and deliberately trespassed. But there was no other choice. I couldn't let them die!"

"She speaks the truth," Mandha said. "The females rushed to

the village to call for help. The beasts were after my mate and child."

"Salha?!" I exclaimed.

"Yes. They are shaken, but fine," Mandha said.

"You see?" the human said, hope blossoming in her golden eyes, the color of honey, and a slightly paler shade than her brown skin. "I meant no offense and no disrespect. I just wanted to help. I'm a hunter. I knew I could save them."

"Be that as it may, she has trespassed," Raskier said. "The rules are the rules."

Although prone to kill first and ask questions later, Raskier turned to look at me with a questioning look. Every other eye turned to me.

"Yes, the rules are the rules," I conceded.

"Are you serious?" the female exclaimed, her gaze flicking through each of our faces before settling on mine. "You want to punish me for saving your people? For saving his mate?"

"If we *wanted* to kill you for this, you would already be dead," I said in a neutral tone. "But you have trespassed. Extenuating circumstances or not, letting you go without repercussions will create a dangerous precedent with potentially serious consequences. This is a decision for the Elders to make. You will surrender your weapons and follow us peacefully to the village."

She opened and closed her mouth a few times, as if looking for the words to argue. I gave her a stern look, making it clear this wasn't open for discussion. Her shoulders slouched, defeated. She removed her belt, the crossbolt on her back, and the weapons pouch hanging below her speeder's handles and handed them over to Raskier and Mandha.

"We will not shackle you, and allow you to travel on your own speeder," I said calmly. "But try to flee and things will become a lot less pleasant."

"I'm not going to run. If that had been my intention, I would have already done it," she replied stiffly. "I'm not a bad person."

Pride and something akin to anger had seeped into her voice, replacing her fear. That rekindled the fascination she had awakened in me. Our females didn't battle. They'd laugh at us for even suggesting they could try to hunt. I'd observed this delicate human on a few occasions throughout the day. She'd impressed me with her efficiency, working around her limitations to make reasonably clean kills, nothing like the butchery she'd made of these two Flayers.

"And if I believed you were, things would be going down quite differently," I said.

Without waiting for her to respond, I turned to my Drayshan, Dagas. Using one of the three short and recurved bone spikes on its side as support, I hoisted myself into the recess on its back, lying on my stomach and wrapping my tail around his hind horn. Thanks to its shorter back legs, we were lying at a 30-degree angle on the beast, its flat head giving us a clear view ahead. I closed my hands around two of the horns protruding from the sides of its neck before casting a glance at the female.

That seemed to snap her out of the daze she'd appeared to have fallen into while observing me mount. She got onto her own transportation and quietly followed as we raced home.

A million troubling thoughts went off in my mind. The female didn't deserve to die, especially not after saving my brother's mate and child. When she'd stumbled upon the first Flayer we'd killed, I'd wondered if she'd been the Zamorian's acolyte. However, her surprise and then hesitation at claiming it had been genuine. With our camouflage, she hadn't seen us watching her. But it wasn't until she'd shown herself after observing us performing that kill, then congratulating us for it, that she truly piqued my curiosity.

Although I'd derived a malicious glee at watching her unknowingly 'steal' the Zamorian's would-be kills, that hadn't been the main reason I'd dragged that dead Flayer out of the restricted area so that she could claim it. If I were honest with myself, I'd wanted an excuse to see her up-close and talk to her —not that I'd done much of the latter. I'd been too busy taking in her appearance and tasting her scent.

Of all the species visiting us, hers had the most in common with ours. Although our females didn't have prominent breasts like humans, they had the same slender and delicate upper-body constitution. She had harmonious features and was pleasant to the eyes. A hood instead of the black, curly hair on her head would have made her stunning. Like all the members of her species that I'd seen up to now, she wore far too much body covering. I could only see the golden-brown skin on her face and the back of her hands. She was otherwise hidden by dark leather that stuck closely to her sensuous curves, even her legs. Had she been Ordosian, the color of her scales—based on her skin coloration—would have been breathtaking.

And a tail instead of those weird legs would have made her perfect.

However, all those wandering thoughts faded, my insides twisting with worry as the trees parted to reveal the village. I flicked my tongue out a couple of times, tasting the human's growing fear. It had dampened during our journey here, but now, her fate would be decided.

The tribe had gathered on the square, the three Elders waiting by the statue of Isshaya, the Great Goddess, who watched over our people. The crowd parted, moving to the sides of the square to make way for us. I stopped my mount on the grassy area a couple of meters away from the stone-paved square. To my relief, the human imitated me. She dismounted at the same time I did, her worried gaze weighing heavily on me. For some irrational reason, I wanted to go to her, take her hand, and tell her all would be well.

I firmly intended for all to be well. She'd saved the life of my nephew and mating-sister. A blood debt had been incurred. My brother and I would see it repaid. I gestured for her to follow me.

She complied, her eyes nervously flicking this way and that, looking at the crowd gathered around us. I couldn't begin to imagine how intimidating this had to be for her. On top of examining her closely, as most of my people had never seen a human in the flesh, everyone was flicking their tongues at her to get additional information. While that was normal for me, I wondered how she perceived it.

Salha pushed forward to be in front of the crowd, her hand resting on the shoulder of little Eicu. The youngling had only seen five summers, and yet he was already quite the handful.

We stopped a couple of meters in front of the Elders.

"Elder Krathi," I said, bowing my head to the female in the middle, effectively the leader of our tribe, "Elder Jyotha," I said, repeating the gesture towards the female on her right, and second in command, "Elder Iskal, I said, saluting the male on her left.

The human cast a nervous glance towards me the minute I started talking, then also bowed her head to each of the Elders when I did: a sensible and clever gesture that didn't go unnoticed.

"Great Hunter Szaro, you've brought back the intruder alive and unbound," Elder Krathi responded in Universal, her gaze locked on the female.

The human shuddered and cast a panicked look towards me. Thankfully, she held her tongue. The factual and calm voice the Elder spoke with gave me hope Salha's report of being saved by the human had predisposed the Elder to a more peaceful resolution.

"We have," I replied in a firm and stoic tone. "As my brother's mate likely already related to you, the human trespassed in order to save her life and that of her offspring Eicu. We have observed the human female throughout the day. Not once had she violated our edict until she saw two of ours in distress. As no greed or ill-intent motivated this offense, we felt it better to submit the case to your wisdom."

"We have indeed heard of the rescue," Elder Krathi said. "Tell me human, did your Federation not warn you of the consequences for trespassing?"

"Serena… my name is Serena, Elder Krathi," the female said nervously. "And yes, they warned us, which is why I respected your rules until I could no longer. Leaving a mother and her young child to die when I possess the skill to save them would have been morally wrong."

I didn't know whether to be impressed or cringe at her 'correcting' the Elder by giving her name. And yet, that boldness held the same inexplicable appeal I'd felt when she'd congratulated us earlier. However, the polite tone of her voice, and her correctly remembering Elder Krathi's name and pronouncing it flawlessly, earned her some favor with our leader.

"Even at the cost of your life?" the Elder insisted.

"It shouldn't be one or the other," the human… Serena countered, a sliver of outrage seeping into her voice. "Would you have preferred I'd left them to die?"

"Of course not," Elder Krathi said with a dismissive gesture of the hand.

"And yet, I've been brought before you to be punished for doing the right thing," Serena argued.

"You've been brought before us to see if there's any way you can be spared," Elder Krathi replied, her tone hardening.

"Why does it have to be such a big deal?" Serena asked, clearly confused. "Why can't you just let me go?"

"Because the other off-worlders that have come here with you for the First Hunt have been pushing, testing how far they can go, and how much they can get away with," Elder Jyotha said in a gentle voice. "The Zamorian luring Flayers to our borders for our males to do the work on his behalf is only one of the many offenses the other participants have perpetrated so far."

"But *I* have nothing to do with that!" Serena justly argued.

"You don't," Elder Iskal conceded. "However, regardless of

your altruistic reasons, *you* committed the most grievous one. The map that the Federation provided you also includes a tracker that allows them AND us to know where a hunter has been. The minute you crossed into the forbidden lands, we were warned at the same time they were. By now, everyone at your base camp is aware that one of the hunters has violated the primordial rule. How we respond to that will impact how much bolder they may become."

"But my reasons for doing so—"

"Will only open the door for every trespasser to pretend they, too, had selfless reasons to do so," Elder Krathi interrupted, gently but firmly. "We do not wish you harm… Serena. But we have greater things to take into consideration for the good of our people as a whole. Any resolution to this situation will need to be a deterrent to others."

"Elder Krathi," Mandha intervened, even as I opened my mouth to argue as well, "a blood debt has been incurred. Two of them as a matter of fact." My brother gestured at his son and mate. "There must be an acceptable solution for the human, Serena."

"We understand your situation, Hunter Mandha," Elder Krathi said. "The decision will not be made today. Serena is to be detained until we have discussed the situation with the representative of the United Planets Organization who will be here in the morning."

"You have reached out to the UPO?" Serena asked, stunned but her face filled with hope.

"No, Serena. *You* did through your Federation," the Elder replied.

"I did?" Serena asked, with a confused expression. Then she froze. Her face jerked towards the camera on her shoulder as understanding dawned on her. "Right… I guess I did."

"It was wise to record your actions," Elder Krathi continued. "Let us hope for a good resolution."

CHAPTER 4
SERENA

To say that I was freaking out qualified as the understatement of the year. This had not gone down *at all* as I had hoped. What a fucking nightmare. At least, three things gave me hope. Number one, the two brothers, Szaro and Mandha seemed determined to save me. Second, the Elders didn't seem in a rush to kill me—although I had no doubt they would without hesitation if they failed to find a more acceptable solution for me. And third, the UPO…

When I'd sent that video to the Federation, I had genuinely believed I would have made it back out of the Ordosian territory without getting caught. There had been no warriors in sight. I hadn't known for sure that they could track us, but it made sense in case one of us never returned, so that they could recover our remains—assuming there were any to be found. But that the United Planets Organization got involved spoke volumes about their desire to maintain a peaceful relationship with the Ordosians.

This intergalactic coalition regulated not only inter-planetary trading, but also diplomatic conflict. Planets considered primitive, like Trangor, fell under their protection. As the most advanced species on this planet had not yet achieved interstellar travel capacity, they never should have been exposed to our existence, as per the Prime Directive. A scientific expedition had discreetly come here to retrieve plant and animal samples for pharmaceutical research, discovering a treasure trove that would revolutionize the medical industry.

However, the scientists' efforts at camouflage were easily thwarted by the Ordosians' almost supernatural sensory abilities. Half of the crew was slaughtered, the others barely escaping with their lives. It took a few years of careful observation to learn their language, followed by even more cautious contacts that evolved into intense negotiations before the natives began opening up to possible collaborations with consortiums affiliated with the UPO.

And now, they're coming here to negotiate my release.

There was something bigger at play here than met the eye. I didn't know what it was, but I welcomed it all the same. If the UPO had wanted to sacrifice me for the greater good, I'd be dead already. They wouldn't waste time and resources flying someone all the way here to Trangor.

After the Elders dismissed us, the Great Hunter took me to some kind of a house. Then again, studio would probably be more accurate as it only possessed a single room carved directly into the mountain that surrounded the village. In my distress, I'd failed to take a proper look at the village I'd landed in. The room had been barren aside from a table with a jug of water and an empty glass. In the back corner of the room, a large, square plate appeared embedded in the floor. A huge window let the daylight in but was positioned in such a way that it didn't give me a proper view of any activity in the village.

"You will remain here until the Elders have conferred with your representative tomorrow," Szaro said with his exotic voice. "Do not try to escape. If you require anything, wave your hand in front of that sensor by the door. Someone will come as quickly as possible."

"Okay, but… hmm… any chance I could get a chair and a bed?" I asked.

"Oh yes! Humans require seating furniture," Szaro nodded, looking a little embarrassed. He waved at his lower body and tail. "As you can guess, we do not have chairs. But we will bring you something that can serve that purpose. What is a bed?"

I recoiled. No chairs made sense, but no bed?

"The large, thick cushion you sleep on?" I said, as if it was self-evident.

His slitted eyes flitted to the plate on the floor in the corner of the room. "We sleep on heating plates," he said.

"Right… Well, any chance I could recover some of the things in my backpack and in the storage of my speeder? I have food, an inflatable mattress, and my water purifying pills in there," I said.

"The water provided is safe for you to drink," Szaro said, indicating the pitcher on the table. "And yes, all non-weapon items can be brought to you. However, we will have to rummage through them to sort what you can and cannot have."

I haaaated when people sifted through my shit. It made me feel violated. But under the circumstances, it made sense they would have to do so. I gave him a stiff nod.

"Very well. I will go take care of it," Szaro said.

He turned and slithered towards the door.

"Szaro!" I called out as he reached for the door. He looked at me questioningly over his shoulder. "What's going to happen to me?"

A strange expression flitted over his alien features. "I will not give you an answer that I do not possess, but I promise to make sure we will find an acceptable solution," he answered.

The sincerity in his voice had a soothing effect that took me by surprise. I locked gazes with him, and he held mine unwaveringly. Something settled inside of me, and to my shock, a timid smile stretched my lips.

"Thank you for standing up for me out there," I said in a soft voice.

The same odd expression flitted over his face.

"No, Serena. Thank *you* for saving my mating-sister and nephew," Szaro said.

With a final smile, he exited the room that served me as a cell. Twenty minutes later, a knock on the door startled me. Two males entered carrying a square block of wood with a cushion on top that would serve me as a chair, my backpack, and my mattress. I muttered a thank you. They nodded and left without a word.

After I set up my mattress, snacked on an energy bar, and washed it down with some water, I began the long waiting game as the day stretched endlessly.

I didn't recall falling asleep, only that I performed a lot of tossing and turning. I woke up early, only to find quite a few people in the village had already stirred as well. I couldn't see them, but I could hear some muffled sounds. As I'd realized last night, to my dismay, the room didn't contain a hygiene room. Thankfully, I hadn't drunk too much water. That didn't mean my bladder wouldn't complain at some point. With luck, the UPO representative would have me out of here long before it became a problem.

Being used to roughing it, I pulled out a piece of cloth from my backpack and poured some water from the pitcher to wash the sleep from my face. As the seconds stretched into minutes and then into hours, I fought the urge to call someone by waving my hand in front of the sensor. They'd come for me when they were ready. Still, it confused me that, after the relative kindness they had shown me under the circumstances, they utterly failed as hosts. Nobody came to ask me if I needed food, to use the bathroom, if I was bored—which I obviously was—or if I was simply doing okay. They had confiscated my bracer and datapad, which left me with nothing but my very worried thoughts.

Meditating only helped for so long, and pressing my ear to the door didn't allow me to overhear anything intelligible. The Ordosians would likely speak in their own language anyway, which I obviously didn't understand. After a bit of pacing, I finally settled onto the improvised chair they'd brought me and ate one of my energy bars, both to silence my burgeoning hunger, and to give myself something to do. I was chewing my fourth bite when a solid knock on the door scared the living daylights out of me. I nearly choked on my food, yet managed to bid them come in.

I jumped to my feet, still slightly coughing, my heart pounding as I gazed upon Szaro's solemn face as he entered the room. He stared at me with a strange expression. I gave him a nervous smile to which he responded with a nod before waving someone in. I stretched my neck to look behind him. My jaw dropped at the sight of a Temern.

He resembled a humanoid bird of paradise, with golden feathers, maroon wings, and a long, fluffy white tail. The members of his species were highly respected empaths hired as moderators by major corporations, planetary governments and, of course, the United Planets Organization. Whatever was going on with my situation, it was bigger than I'd realized. You didn't send a Temern to negotiate the release of a hunter of average fame.

"Hello, Ms. Bello. I am Kayog Voln, the negotiator sent by the UPO to handle your situation."

"Hello, Master Voln. But please, call me Serena," I said with a smile.

"Only if you call me Kayog," he replied in the gentle, musical tone that was common to his people.

Although he returned my smile, his beak-like mouth gave it a stiffness that might have been unsettling if not for the kind glimmer in his eyes. Before I could answer, the same male that had brought me my belongings last night brought in a second makeshift chair, which he placed across the table from me.

"Thank you, Irco," Kayog said to the Ordosian male, who nodded in response before leaving.

My brows shot up. Kayog had only gotten here and was already on a first name basis with the locals?

He must have been here before.

It would make sense for them to send someone who already had a good rapport with the Ordosians to help make the negotiations go more smoothly.

"I will leave you to discuss in private," Szaro said, that same enigmatic expression on his face, giving me the heebie-jeebies. "I will be right outside when you are done."

He exchanged a glance with Kayog, who raised his feathery eyebrows questioningly. Szaro nodded in the way one does to confirm that the plan, challenging though it may be, would proceed as agreed upon. He then left the room without another word. My head jerked towards the Temern, and I forced myself to silence my growing panic.

"Is this when I start freaking out?" I asked.

"No, Serena. There is no need for that," Kayog said in a soothing voice while taking a seat. "Please," he added, gesturing to my seat.

I sat down and clasped my hands on the table to keep them from shaking.

His wings shifted as he, too, crossed his hands on the table. "I know you're extremely stressed out over this situation, so I'm going to get straight to the point," Kayog said in a calm voice. "There is a single way out of your current predicament. Unfortunately, it will not be negotiable. While they wish you no harm, the Ordosian leaders are adamant that this one rule be upheld. Any stranger who enters their forbidden lands without express consent forfeits their life. But there is a loophole. If you become Ordosian, you're no longer a trespasser."

My jaw dropped, and my eyes nearly popped out of my head. "Oh, my God! That's so fucking simple!" I exclaimed with a nervous laughter. "So… what do I have to do? Study their culture, their language, their national anthem, and then pass a test? I can do that! I'm a quick study."

Kayog gave me an indulgent smile, although this time it didn't reach his silver eyes.

"I guess not," I said, my shoulders slouching.

"Unfortunately not," he concurred. "There are only two ways to become Ordosian. You must either have one parent who is Ordosian or marry one."

The Temern let the words hang between us. My brain froze, refusing to process their meaning.

"Marriage? Are you serious?" I finally asked.

"I'm afraid so, Serena," he said in a sympathetic voice.

"I'm a human with legs and a womb!" I exclaimed. "They're some kind of Nagas with snake tails who lay eggs."

"Actually, the Ordosians are viviparous," Kayog countered. "Their females carry their offspring to term and give birth to live young."

"Fine, I'll give you that one," I said, waving a dismissive hand. "But we're still not compatible! I mean, for fucks sake, don't snakes have two dicks covered with spikes? I'll be freaking torn to shreds!"

The Temern shifted in his seat. Despite the feathers covering his face, I could tell he was blushing. I almost felt guilty for being so crude to the older male. Despite his youthful appearance, the color of his feathers indicated he was no spring chicken.

"Truth be told, Serena, I do not know what their reproductive organs look like," he confessed. "I have no clue if your species are compatible, but I know that this is the only way we can save your life."

I swallowed hard and ran a nervous hand over my braided hair. I sure as hell wasn't ready to be executed so the Ordosians could make a point. But was being trapped for the rest of my life in a loveless marriage with an incompatible mate any better?

"I know you're overwhelmed. I can feel your distress, but things aren't all that dark," Kayog said. He raised an appeasing hand when I gave him a disbelieving look. "I do not normally handle this type of diplomatic issue. However, after studying your case, my kin and I all agreed this would be the only way to save you, and the Elders said as much when I came to meet them. I am the lead agent of the Prime Mating Agency and an expert in interspecies unions. Szaro is a good male. As an empath, I can tell you that, personality-wise, you two are a perfect match. I had not expected that."

"Szaro? *He* would be my husband?" I asked.

While still freaked out about this whole mess, that news appeased me far more than I'd thought possible.

"Yes," Kayog said with a nod. "Understand that he is making a great sacrifice to save you. Only a small percentage of Ordosians actually marry. Most of them are happy to partner with someone for however long that relationship lasts or simply to have offspring. But marriage is exclusive and for life. As the Great Hunter of the Krada tribe, he is a prime male, highly sought after. By marrying, he forfeits any hope of ever having offspring of his own."

"That's fucked up," I said, my frustration and anger rising. "Why should he make that sacrifice over a blood debt that's not even his own. I saved his sister-in-law and nephew."

"But he is a male of honor and principle, *and* he happens to care for you," Kayog said.

I snorted. "Please, he doesn't know jack shit about me. We talked a couple of times for a hot minute."

"And yet, you fascinate him," Kayog said, matter-of-factly. "And I've felt your response to him when he entered the room. You are not indifferent to Szaro. Speaking with you now, sensing your character, I can reaffirm that you are a perfect personality match."

"Be that as it may, we're probably not physically compatible. And even if we are, I have a life that does not involve settling on a primitive planet. This is a life sentence!"

A frown marred the Temern's brow, and he gave me an intense stare that made me want to squirm in my seat. "While Ordosians marry for life, divorces have occurred in the past, usually because one of the two partners committed a serious offense that got them banned from the tribe. So, if it comes to that, you can divorce him and leave. BUT, as per the Prime Mating Agency rules, if you accept this union, you *must* remain married for at least six months. Normally, we also demand that the marriage be consummated on the wedding night, but in your case, that requirement is permanently waived."

"You're saying that, if I marry him, I don't ever have to sleep with him, and I can divorce him in six months?" I asked, my heart soaring.

By the way the muscles of his jaw tensed, I believed that Kayog was pinching his beak in displeasure, the presumption further confirmed by the lack of warmth in his eyes.

"I'm saying that you will marry a good male who is upending his life to save yours. He will not demand any marital privileges from you. And should both of you truly be miserable in this union, it can be terminated only after a period of at least six months," Kayog said.

"And Szaro agreed to this?" I insisted.

Kayog heaved a sigh. "Yes, he did. But I must caution you. To the entire village, and to the other Ordosian tribes, your union to Szaro will be a real one. Even if you're going into this already planning on leaving in six months, you must play the game until then, and not let it slip in any way. You do not have to pretend to have feelings for him—everyone knows it's not a marriage of love—but you have to act like it's a true union. I cannot predict what backlash may stem from your failure to do so. Can you handle it?"

I nodded. "Yes. Yes, I can do that. But… Why are you doing this? Why are you helping me? What's in it for the UPO?"

Kayog smiled and tilted his head to the side in a way typical of birds. "It has taken years to finally get the Ordosians to warm up to strangers—if we can even call it that," the Temern explained. "The flora and fauna of Trangor is a treasure trove for the medical and pharmaceutical industry. And the Ordosians are their guardians. This is a wild and savage planet. Without the constant vigilance and efforts of these tribes to maintain the balance, swarming beasts like the Flayers would wipe out entire species on this planet, species that can help us produce the cure or treatments for some of the worst diseases in the galaxy. We *need* to maintain a good rapport with the locals and even strengthen that bond. And you can greatly help in that."

"Me?!" I exclaimed, baffled. "I'm just an ex-gymnast turned monster hunter. I'm not a diplomat."

"No, but you have a beautiful soul, great moral values, and a selfless personality," Kayog countered. "That makes you the perfect ambassador to show the Ordosians that off-worlders are not so bad."

"I see," I said, embarrassed by the flurry of compliments. "So… what happens now?"

"Now, I will let you confirm your consent to Szaro. Then we will have an expedited human wedding so that your union can be formally recorded in the galactic registry. We will have all of your personal effects currently at the Federation base camp transferred here, and you can provide me with instructions on getting whatever belongings off-world you would like transported here."

I felt dizzy. This was happening way too fast.

"You are distressed, which is perfectly understandable. But take heart, Serena," Kayog said in a paternal voice that made my throat tighten. "Either way, everything will work out for you in the end. Szaro is a good male. If your union doesn't work out, consider it as you having enjoyed a six-month vacation in the most exclusive resort in the world. No other off-worlder will experience the depth of beauty and wealth of Trangor and its inhabitants."

"True, but that's six months without work or income that I will have to make up for once I'm free," I mumbled, immediately feeling snotty for it.

Yeah, it would make a dent in my nest egg, but it wouldn't put me out on the street. And the thought of truly exploring Trangor in a way no one else ever could held an undeniable appeal. This planet was the Australia of the galaxy. They had the weirdest, most bizarre fauna ever seen, and most of it wanted to kill you just for fun.

The Temern grinned, his silver eyes lighting up. "Actually, you shouldn't be hurting too badly. You will still be compensated for all the kills you have performed so far as part of the First Hunt. Furthermore, as punishment for luring Flayers, endangering the local population, and indirectly causing your current predicament, the Zamorian name Bayrohnziyiek Skortheatis has been stripped of all of his claimed 'kills' alongside the Krada tribe's border. Instead, they have been attributed to you and added to your personal score, which puts you squarely in the lead at the present time. On top of that, once your situation here has been ironed out with the Elders of the tribe, you are free to resume the hunt."

"Are you serious?!" I exclaimed, my mind reeling. Even if I ended up being knocked from first place, that would still put me in a very comfortable financial situation once I regained my freedom.

"I am. BUT, keep in mind that your freedom of movement will likely be restricted for the first few weeks," Kayog warned. "Everyone knows you're not happily entering into this union. They will not give you an easy way to flee, or be tempted to do so. It would create a very difficult diplomatic situation for us."

"Don't worry," I said with a stiff nod. "I will hold my end of the deal. Anyway, if I ran, the UPO and the Federation would make me rue the day I reneged on the agreement."

"I'm glad we understand each other," Kayog said with an approving nod. "Do you have any other questions?"

"Oh, I'm sure there are a million more that will pop up once you're gone, but for now, I really just want to get this thing done," I said honestly, feeling a little dejected. "I'll remain stressed as hell until that scary Elder Krathi says that I'm a member of the tribe and that the threat hanging over my head has been lifted."

"Very well. While they may seem primitive on the surface, and technically are by galactic standards, the Ordosians possess a great deal of technology, including long-range com systems. You will be able to contact me if you need anything, although there may be a few hours of delay before I receive your message and before my answer reaches you."

"Thank you, Kayog," I said with genuine gratitude. "Thanks for saving my ass."

"Remember to thank Szaro, as well," the agent said in a soft voice. "Without him, we could not have saved you."

"I will not forget," I assured him.

He smiled, rose to his feet, and went to knock on the door. It opened almost instantly. Szaro glanced at me before looking at Kayog inquisitively. The agent nodded in response to his unspoken question. To my shock, the Ordosian's shoulders almost imperceptibly relaxed with what I could only interpret as relief. Had he feared I would refuse?

Kayog left the room and Szaro glided in, coming to a stop in front of me. I made to stand up, but he gestured for me to remain seated. His tail wrapped behind him neatly in a tight S and he lowered himself onto it, in the equivalent of a sitting position that put him almost at eye-level with me. We stared at each other quietly for a few seconds. He seemed to be searching for what to say just like I was.

"Thank you for volunteering for this to save my life," I said at last.

"I promised we would find a solution," he replied gently.

"But at what cost to you?" I asked.

He didn't respond at first, his reptilian eyes studying my features. "Time will tell. We are not a traditional couple, but stranger things have happened."

I stiffened upon hearing those words. Although Kayog had hinted at this, Szaro's underlying meaning made it clear we needed to openly express our mutual expectations before entering into any of this. However, even as that thought crossed my mind, a sliver of fear blossomed inside of me. I didn't want to mislead him about the fact I intended to haul ass out of here the minute the six months were up. But what if that made him rescind his offer to marry me?

Kayog said he agreed...

His tongue flicked, and his eyes narrowed, making my anxiety go up a notch.

"I can taste the worry my words have stirred in you," Szaro said. "I am taking you as my mate, Serena Bello. Ordosians bind for life. I have no control over what you will do, only over my own actions. Therefore, I will endeavor to be the best possible mate for you for as long as I draw breath, or until such time as you decide I'm not worthy."

"It has nothing to do with your worth," I argued softly. "By your actions so far, you've proven to be an upstanding male. But we are completely different species and probably not compatible."

"I believe that we are far more compatible than you think, Serena," Szaro said with that sexy underlying rattling sound in his voice. "There will be plenty of time for us to discover it. As odd as I may look to you, I know that you do not find me repulsive. I find you pleasing to the eye, and your unusual hunter nature for a female intrigues me. I expect nothing from you that you are unwilling to give. I only ask that you keep an open mind, be loyal to your new people, and adapt to our ways. And if you do not find happiness here, I will not hold you against your will."

"That's… that's more than fair. And yes, I can do that," I said, my cheeks burning to learn that he'd realized I had enjoyed the view.

"Then we are in agreement. Come, my mate," Szaro said, straightening up. "Let us get you out of this room and finalize the binding ritual of your people. Tonight, we will be bound according to the Ordosian ways."

My stomach quivered upon hearing the possessive way in which he called me his mate. It should freak me out. This entire mess of a situation should have me running around screaming like a madwoman. And yet, Szaro had an uncanny way of making me feel safe, like everything would be just fine. Rising from my chair, I followed him out towards the crazy destiny that awaited us.

CHAPTER 5
SZARO

While I spoke with my mate, Elder Krathi had given permission to a human official to fly into Krada. On top of bringing Serena's belongings from the Federation base camp, he was apparently also legally authorized to preside over human bindings. Kayog had warned me we would only experience the expedited form of their ritual, giving me a quick overview of the process. I just never imagined it would be this dismissive.

As I stood face to face with Serena on the square in front of the statue of the Goddess, the male standing next to us asked that we repeat after him.

"Serena Bello, do you freely take this Ordosian male, Szaro Kota, as your lawfully wedded husband?" he asked.

"I do," Serena replied.

"Szaro Kota, do you freely take this human female, Serena Bello, as your lawfully wedded wife?" he then asked me.

"I do," I replied.

"Kayog Voln, do you confirm bearing witness to Serena Bello and Szaro Kota freely exchanging their desire to be legally married to each other?"

"Yes, I confirm it," Kayog said.

"By the power vested in me by the United Planets Organization, I declare you husband and wife," the male said. "Congratulations, you may kiss the bride."

Although shocked by the brevity of this ceremony—if it could even qualify as that—I repressed a smile. Earlier, Kayog had explained kissing to me, which I was familiar with since Ordosian practiced it. Apparently, as that had tripped a number of mates he'd paired with humans in the past, he now made sure to warn them to avoid future awkwardness when the officiant requested they do so. My mate lifted her face towards me, her expression unreadable as I leaned forward to press my lips against hers.

They were pleasantly soft and warm, just like the palm she pressed on my chest, as if for support. Serena's touch was fleeting, as was the kiss. Before I could properly savor the sensation, my mate pulled away from me, and gave me a timid smile. I instinctively flicked my tongue, tasting her response. Although she tried to hide it, my tongue bothered my mate. And yet, it constituted an integral part of me and of my species as a whole that she would need to grow used to. And in her presence, my tongue constantly itched to come out.

Her scent tasted exquisite. Delicate and fresh, like the clean air of the early hours of a sunny day, before the morning dew evaporated from the leaves and before the wind mixed the scent of the waking world into a big melting pot. And underneath it all, that tiny drop of heat, the same one that had emanated from Serena the first time we spoke by the border, after I brought the dead Flayer to her. Her timid attraction to me taunted me in the most peculiar fashion. I intended to savor it in its fullness, once Serena shed her thoughts of leaving and began embracing our union.

"Please sign here," the human male said, snapping me out of my musings.

Serena pressed her thumb in the box on the interface of the

male's datapad. I repeated her gesture in the neighboring box once she was done.

"Congratulations again," the male said, putting away the datapad in the satchel hanging on his hips. "I wish you both the very best."

Although he spoke to both of us, the way his gaze lingered on Serena expressed clearly he thought she would be miserable. That angered me. While I probably never would have even contemplated pursuing a human female in a romantic fashion, Serena was my mate now, and I intended to make this permanent.

"Thank you," Serena responded gently.

I merely nodded and turned my gaze to the three Elders standing nearby.

"Congratulations, Serena and Szaro on your union. And welcome, Serena Bello, to the Krada tribe of Trangor and to the great Ordosian family," Elder Krathi said. "Tonight, we will celebrate your union according to our tradition so that you may officially become part of the people."

"Thank you, Elder Krathi," Serena said politely.

The other Elders smiled at us before leaving, the rest of the tribe who had come to bear witness also scattering with the same unimpressed expression on their faces. Tonight would make up for it.

After exchanging goodbyes with Kayog, I picked up the two large bags containing Serena's meager belongings from the base camp.

"I will take you to our dwelling," I said, my hood itching to shrink with embarrassment.

While I had secured a prime location for my dwelling, it was nowhere near ready for a mate. Over the years, I had imagined how I would painstakingly build the perfect nest for my mate, designed specifically for her as a testament of how well I knew and adored her—an understanding acquired over months, if not years, of assiduous courtship. Instead, I was welcoming a mate I didn't know and barely understood into the barebone canvas of a home.

As with most premium estates, mine was carved directly into the mountain that offered natural protection on two sides of the village, framed to the north by the Bayagi River.

"I'm afraid my dwelling isn't prepared for a mate, let alone a human one," I said apologetically, as I opened the door. "You must tell me what you require, and I'll see to it as quickly as possible. For now, I've asked Irco to bring you these couple of chairs," I said waving at them next to the large stone table that occupied the space in front of the sink near the large windows.

Serena nodded absentmindedly while her gaze roamed over the otherwise barren room. The light grey stone of the walls, almost white, had not been perfectly polished and smoothed as they would be reworked once I knew what type of design would suit my mate. The floor, too, was a little rough, although very clean. No decoration adorned the walls, no shelves displayed trophies or mementos. The only things to see in the room aside from the table and two newly added makeshift chairs, were the sink and the two glasses on the shelf above it.

Despite her best effort to keep a neutral expression, Serena couldn't have been less impressed.

"The rest room is this way," I said, dying with embarrassment, irrational though it was. Negligence wasn't the reason for my dwelling being this bare.

"A restroom?! You have one here?" she exclaimed, her face lighting with a mix of relief and delight.

While her reaction pleased me, it also seriously confused me. Why wouldn't I have a place to rest?

"Yes, this way," I said, gesturing at the first door to the left of the hallway from the main room.

I opened the door and led her in. As soon as she entered the room, her face fell.

"Oooh, a rest room, not a restroom," she said, scrunching her face.

I blinked, not understanding how putting a longer pause between the two words made a difference.

"What were you expecting instead?" I asked, confused by her reaction.

"I thought you were referring to the hygiene room, which is what we call a restroom… one word," Serena explained. She then indicated the room. "This is what we would call a bedroom. But then, you guys don't have beds," she added, casting a glance at my heating plate.

"Oh, we have a hygiene space," I replied with a sliver of relief.

"You do?" Serena asked, turning to look out the open door.

"Yes, but not inside this dwelling," I amended. Her shoulders drooped, disappointment seeping back on her face. That stung. "I will show you where it is after we are done here. This chest of drawers contains my adornments," I continued pointing at it. "Irco will bring one for you in the next hour. You can also give him the description of all the furniture you require for sleeping, and sitting, or anything else."

"Okay, that would be nice," she said with a grateful smile.

"Please do not be disheartened by finding this dwelling so inadequate," I said, holding her gaze unwaveringly. "This barren state is normal for a non-mated, non-paired Ordosian male. We prepare the nest specifically for the female we chose over the long period of courtship, which you and I didn't have. For now, I can only get you the essentials so that you can function. I will make this dwelling worthy of you over the days and weeks to come."

Serena shifted on her feet, a guilty expression descending on her features. "You don't have to go out of your way. Seriously. I… I'm sorry if my reaction made you feel bad or embarrassed about your home," she said with a sheepish smile. "I know nothing of your people. You're the first sentient species with a tail instead of legs that I've interacted with. But I'm realizing now that, beyond our physical differences, your culture is even more foreign to me than what I could have imagined."

"Based on what little I've seen so far of human culture, I agree that you will have a great deal to adapt to. But I will help you through that," I said with a smile.

"I appreciate it. I only ask that you be patient with me and especially that you do not take offense at my reactions," Serena added, making a strange expression. "I have an excessively expressive face, and looking at me, you'd always think things are far worse than they truly are. So, don't get discouraged either if I look depressed or upset. It's just my face being silly. If there is truly a problem, I *will* speak up."

"Good, I'm glad to hear it."

"Which brings us back to this furniture stuff," Serena continued. "You don't need to have anything fancy made for me. I'm a simple girl. I'm used to roughing it out in the woods. Functional is good enough for—"

"No," I interrupted sternly, making her recoil in surprise. "You are my mate. You will get nothing less than the best. That is *not* negotiable," I added when she opened her mouth to argue. "Come, let me show you the rest."

She made a face at me that seemed to hint this discussion wasn't over but complied as I led her across the hallway to the door facing our rest room.

"This is the only other room that isn't completely empty in this dwelling," I said while opening the door.

I didn't know what reaction I had expected from Serena, but not for her jaw to drop and her eyes to fill with stars as she gazed upon the contents of the room. The look of wonder on her alien —but pretty—face sent the most pleasant shiver down my scales.

"Holy cow! This is freaking amazing!" Serena whispered.

She slowly stepped inside the armory, her eyes flicking in

every direction to admire my weapons. She would stop only for a moment to gape at a bow, a dagger, or a spear, before moving on to the next table or rack.

"You can touch," I said, pleased beyond words by her reaction to my greatest pride. Ordosian females had little interest in hunting gear.

"Really?!" she asked, beaming at me. When I nodded, she replied, "Thank you!"

And touch she did, with a gentle caress from the tips of her dainty fingers or the brush of her knuckles. My mate handled my weapons with the care and reverence of a lover… as it should be.

"This is exquisite craftsmanship," she said with undisguised admiration.

"Thank you," I said, puffing out my chest.

Her head jerked towards me, and she gave me a stunned look. "You made them?"

I nodded. "Yes, my mate. Every single weapon in this room, I made with my own hands."

"Any chance I can bribe you into letting me use them one of these days?" she asked, batting her eyes in the oddest, yet most adorable fashion.

I smiled. "That could be arranged," I replied, happy we had found a common ground—our first, I hoped. My mind was already bursting with ideas of weapons I could craft for her. "Come, let me show you the rest of the house."

She nodded and cast one last awed look at my armory before following me into the hallway.

"There are seven more rooms, which can be reshaped if needed," I said while giving her a glimpse of them. "They were originally meant as rest rooms for my future offspring, a playroom or study room, or whatever else my mate would have seen fit. Think of what you would like to do with the space."

I didn't miss the way she frowned—before quickly hiding it —when I mentioned offspring. I'd always wanted younglings, at least two, but more like four or five, hence the large number of rooms. Since the birth of Mandha's son, Eicu, that desire had grown even stronger. On a few occasions, I'd seriously considered siring a young on one of the many non-mated females of the tribe that had expressed their interest in bearing my offspring. But I'd resisted the temptation as I'd wanted to raise my younglings in my own dwelling that I would share with their mother, my bonded mate.

I gave Serena a sideways glance. I didn't know if we were compatible. Humans carried their young to term just like our females. But assuming my seed could even take root in her womb, what would our offspring look like? The picture of a young hunter, with golden brown scales the color of Serena's skin, her harmonious features, a long, thick tail, and as wide a hood as mine popped in my mind. I silenced the violent longing that struck me. My mate was nowhere near ready to even consider laying with me—assuming we were compatible. And even if we did and managed to conceive, there was a real possibility our offspring would come out looking human with legs.

And I would still love it and happily welcome it.

That realization pleased me as much as it stunned me. I had six months to convince my mate to make our bonding work, and I fully intended to succeed, as I normally did with all of my endeavors.

"This is the terrace," I said, opening the large door at the back of the dwelling.

"Oh. My. God!" she whispered when I moved aside to let her out.

Serena froze and gaped in disbelief and wonder at the breathtaking view of the hidden valley inside of the mountain, of the two waterfalls, and of the river that ran 75 meters below. A thick stone railing delimited the large balcony that measured ten meters wide and five meters deep. Birds added their voices to the hum of the waterfalls as a variety of peaceful herbivores roamed around the shore below.

My mate approached the railing, walking with a dazed expression as she took in her surroundings.

"This is a true paradise," she said. "It's beyond enchanting. It's mesmerizing."

"I am happy you like it," I said, making no effort to hide how much her reaction pleased me.

"There are no words to describe just how much I love it," she said.

"And this is but the first of the many wonders of your new world that I will show you," I said shamelessly.

She snorted, immediately understanding my less-than-subtle underlying message by referring to this as *her* new world.

"I look forward to it," she replied with a smile.

"There is a hover platform and a hidden path accessible through here to go down to the river," I said, pointing at the barely noticeable gate in the back corner of the railing. "In the upcoming days, I will take you down for a walk in the valley. It is a sanctuary where we shelter very unique but peaceful creatures that would otherwise face extinction had they remained in their natural habitats. Trangor is a dangerous place."

"That will be awesome," Serena said with a spark in her eyes that ignited a pleasant heat in the pit of my stomach.

I loved pleasing my mate.

"This concludes the tour of the house. I will now take you to the hygiene area," I said.

"Wait," Serena said with a frown. "I didn't see any kitchen or cooking area. No fridge, cooling units, or larder. There's only the sink for water in what I'm guessing is the dining area at the entrance. I mean, no hygiene room is strange enough, but no kitchen? Don't you get hungry?"

"Ordosians have no need to dedicate an entire room in each of their dwellings for such things," I explained with a slight frown of my own. "If a room isn't going to be used daily or at least every two or three days, there's no point having it in a house."

"Well, don't you have to eat every day, and relieve yourself of all the things you eat at least a couple of times a day?" She asked, flabbergasted.

"Every day? Thankfully no. Do you?"

"Yes!" Serena exclaimed. "Humans normally eat three meals a day, not to mention the snacks in between. And we use the hygiene room on average as many times daily. Some people even more frequently than that."

I stared at my female in horror. "THREE? Goddess… We haven't fed you since midday yesterday. We've starved you and deprived you of relief! I am so sorry, my mate! I did not know. Why didn't you speak up? I will fetch sustenance for you at once. What do—?"

"No, no, Szaro, I'm fine," she interrupted while placing a soothing palm on my bare chest. "I had some energy bars in my backpack. I ate some yesterday, and another for breakfast this morning. I won't be hungry for another couple of hours. However, my bladder isn't too happy with me right now and could really use a break. So, visiting that hygiene room some time really soon would be a good idea."

"Of course, my mate. This way," I said, leading the way back out of the dwelling through the front entrance. "After that, we can look into addressing your nutritional needs."

"How often do Ordosians eat?" Serena asked as we exited the dwelling.

"I tend to eat once every two or three weeks, unless I am heading out on a long ranging expedition. In that case, I eat a very large meal that can hold me up to a month," I explained as I led her through the square and down the path to the northeast that opened onto the hygiene cave, almost beneath the waterfall. "I will not need sustenance for another couple of weeks.

Younglings eat more often. Little ones, like my nephew Eicu, must eat at least once a week, although it tends to be closer to once every four or five days. Younger ones will eat small meals every other day."

"Wow, I guess it must be convenient to not have to worry about food for weeks when you're out on the trail," she said, eyeing me with incredulity. "So much for family dinners," she mumbled under her breath.

I opened my mouth to respond, but my mate's gasp silenced me. I loved the way her face lit up as she discovered my world. While I understood her reaction on the terrace overlooking the river, this struck me as amusing. People rarely stared in awe at the cleansing room. It was basic, and functional—a place where you scrubbed the dirt off your body and emptied your bowels. Still, it forced me to look at it with new eyes.

The natural cave of pale stones had many openings in the ceiling through which water rained down, allowing for at least fifty people to shower at the same time. The water pooled on the recessed ground, ten centimeters deep, and deep grooves on an incline, narrow enough to allow us to slither over them, drained the water towards the large window at the back of the cave so that it could fall out through the bars of the protective railing. The view onto the valley from here was once more stunning. Glowstones embedded in the walls illuminated the space.

"This is gorgeous," Serena said with sincere admiration. "You guys really know how to leverage the beauty of nature."

"We are its guardian," I said, puffing out my chest.

I advanced into the water and gestured for her to follow. She hesitated and looked at her feet.

"Are you afraid to wet your shoes?" I asked.

"No. These boots are waterproof," she replied, shaking her head. "I just don't want to sully the water."

I laughed. "Once the water hits the ground, it is considered wastewater that gets filtered on its way down to the river in the valley."

"Wastewater?" Serena asked. "But it—"

She froze, her eyes widening as she gave the cleansing room a second look. "Wait, these are your showers? This is like one big communal shower?"

"Yes," I said, confused by her sudden mood swing.

"Yeaaah… No. That's not going to work for me," she said, involuntarily taking a step back. "We don't do public nudity. At least, I don't."

I blinked, then let my gaze roam over her. The majority of her body was indeed covered in leather. Every human I had ever encountered always wore many pieces of clothing, sometimes in multiple layers.

"I realize why this is a non-issue for Ordosians," she said in a reasonable voice. "Your species is essentially always naked. But then, your naughty bits are hidden. With humans, once we take our clothes off, everything is hanging out for the world to gawk at. That's a no-no."

"Naughty bits?" I asked, tilting my head to the side.

"Our genitals," she explained sheepishly.

"All right…" I said slowly, not sure what her point was. "And?"

"And we don't expose ourselves in public. Only to our mate in private," she said. "That's why human dwellings all have at least one, sometimes two or more hygiene rooms. And in public showers, there are usually dividers with curtains or occluding doors so that we can wash in a common setting while preserving our modesty."

"I see," I replied, although I didn't quite get it.

Sure, I understood her words, but failed to see the logic in it. Humans knew how other humans were made, based on their gender. Why hide it from each other? Why only show their genitals to their mate? There was nothing wrong with others seeing, as long as they didn't touch. For many of the species we watched over, flaunting the reproductive attributes of their mates was not only a source of pride but a display of dominance. Only the best male could secure the affections of such a stellar female. But there would be time later for me to inquire further about this odd human behavior.

"If we erect an occluding wall or curtains around one of the water holes, would that work for you?" I asked.

She nodded. "Yes. But there would need to be a bit of space away from the raining water for me to dry myself and get dressed again," she added with an apologetic expression.

"That will be arranged," I said, before glancing at the small amount of skin she had visible. "You must dry? Your skin doesn't shed the water?"

"Not exactly. I mean, water clings to us for a while, although it will evaporate over time if we don't use a towel. But it's even worse with my hair. It will stay wet for hours if I don't dry it," she replied. "Why? Don't you stay wet?"

I shook my head. "Wait, I'll show you."

I moved towards one of the holes and let the water rain down on me. After a few seconds, I returned to my mate. By the time I reached her, almost every drop had already fallen off.

"Are you kidding me?" she whispered as she raised a hand toward me.

My abdominal muscles contracted in anticipation but, to my great disappointment, she stopped herself at the last minute, yanking her hand away. I was curious about the feel of her hand on me, but also about the texture of her soft, scaleless skin.

"Sorry," she said apologetically.

"Do not apologize, Serena," I said in a gentle voice. "I am your mate. You have the right to touch me whenever you please. Go ahead," I said encouragingly.

She hesitated for one more second then proceeded. I barely repressed a shiver as she carefully brushed her fingertips against the scales of my left arm. It tickled in a teasing way. But I wanted a real touch… which she denied me.

"This is really cool," she said, dropping her hand.

Although the term 'cool' sounded strange in this context, I understood her implied meaning.

"The waste chutes are over here," I said, leading her to the waste area on the slightly elevated left side of the cave.

The ground there was dry and a waist-high wall with a holding bar separated it from the cleansing area. In a wide recess on the ground, ten discs, at a two-meter interval from each other, covered the waste holes.

"This is where we empty our cloaca," I explained. "There is a sensor that will open the chute once someone gets in position. Since you don't have a tail, we may need to do some testing to find the right angle for you or make some adjustments for this to work with your anatomy."

The wary look on Serena's face—including a hint of horror —made me realize this would not be well-received either.

"There is enough space between the chutes for us to add a privacy enclosure for you," I added preemptively. Although that appeared to mollify her a bit, my mate still had that 'this-is-absolutely-not-good-for-me' expression on her face. "Let me show you how it works."

I advanced to the edge, where the recess began, then looked at my mate.

"You place your hands on the bar like this for support," I said, doing it at the same time. "As you can see, the disc automatically opens, revealing the chute. As an Ordosian, I only have to advance further to align my cloaca with the hole." Although I didn't need to relieve myself right this instant, I opened my cloaca to show her. "Now, my scales are parted above the chute, and the recess keeps me from entering in contact with it. Once done, I press the interface here on the bar."

I did it, and a strong stream of water shot out, cleansing the opening of my cloaca, the water then falling into the chute. I closed my scales then backed away, the disc closing over the chute as soon as I was far enough.

I single look at my mate's face sufficed for me to know this was *definitely not* going to work.

CHAPTER 6

SERENA

I stared at Szaro in utter and complete shock. On the other side of the room, they had a similar setup with another dozen holes in a small ditch along the elevated area we were standing on. This felt like the Ordosian version of ancient Rome's public latrines. The only two differences were that the locals were standing instead of sitting, and that they had a fancy bidet instead of the sponge sticks the Romans washed their asses with.

"Okay… So… even with privacy walls, this is NOT going to work," I said, still reeling from the fact that, for a moment, I thought my brand-new husband was going to take a shit right in front of me. Of all the things *not* to do on a first date, that most definitely qualified as it. Thankfully, he had not. "Humans require a seat with a hole in the middle for that. We don't crouch over holes like that, unless we're in the middle of the jungle and have to make do. I mean, man can urinate standing up, but for solid waste, they need to sit as well. Women need to sit for both."

Szaro recoiled, looking somewhat confused. "Why do you use different positions? Don't you have a cloaca that handles both? And why isn't it the same for males and females?"

"No," I said, before giving him a quick lesson in human anatomy. "So, crouching over a hole while hanging on to a bar doesn't feature very high on my to do list."

Szaro scratched the inside of his hood while staring at my crotch as if he could see it through my clothes.

"I see," he said in a voice that rather expressed the opposite. "How urgently do you need to relieve yourself right now?"

"It's not yet urgent, but definitely getting there," I said.

"Come, I will take you to Irco. We will quickly devise a solution for you. You will have the waste seat you require," Szaro said in a solemn voice that made me want to chuckle, but also worried me slightly.

He was taking his husband's role *very* seriously. That was a great thing for me, but it concerned me that, the day I left, he would be hurt. Szaro genuinely seemed like a nice guy. Had he been human, I would have liked to date him. I loved the efforts he was making to ensure my comfort. If my stay here had been short, I would have sucked it up and found a discreet spot in the woods to do my business. But six months was far too long to tough it out needlessly.

That said, I would need to rein him in. From the way he spoke, Szaro truly intended to go all out turning his house into my dream home. The selfish part of me wanted to take advantage and see what wonders could be achieved with his cave. The potential certainly was there. And that terrace…! But it would be unfair to him and his true future wife.

As he led me back towards the village square, I finally took a minute to really take in my surroundings. Krada was a sprawling village enclosed by the mountain. In addition to the many dwellings carved directly into the mountain, many other one-story houses framed the square. Built with pale stone, they had a tropical feel to them, the modern and high-tech elements blending in seamlessly. Despite the great deal of vegetation all around, including flowers, trees, and bushes, the Ordosians had not tried to blend the man-made constructions into the environment. They had paved every walkway with stones, bricks, or some sort of pavement.

While they built all the residences in the center around the square, they'd placed the community buildings like their school, library, and entertainment facilities to the left, near the hygiene area. At the other end, on the right side, they'd grouped the commercial buildings. They didn't have a state-of-the-art feel to them. They merely looked like bigger versions of the stone dwellings, except for one massive greenhouse. As we came closer, I realized it was more like an interior garden or atrium as I could see small creatures flying inside. My curiosity was cut short by Irco emerging from a building and coming to meet us halfway.

After quick introductions, Szaro explained some of the things I needed, while I stood there, feeling a little mortified and wondering if the Ordosian builder would think me a diva. To my pleasant surprise, Irco perked up.

"Interesting needs," the builder said with a wide grin. "Let me get a tablet to sketch, and we can go back to the cleansing area to see how we can accommodate you."

"Thank you," I said, relief washing over me.

"We will have everything you need set up in no time," Szaro proudly said as we watched Irco slither back into the building to fetch his tablet. "Irco is very creative and very skilled. Give him a good challenge."

"Oh, I don't want to burden—"

"It is not a burden, my mate," Szaro said firmly, interrupting me. "Beyond the fact that I want the best for you, Irco *will* be happy for it. He loves projects that force him to push himself. He is a little bored with the everyday routine. Give him something to have fun with."

"Well, if you put it like that, I just might," I said.

Szaro beamed at me. It really softened his alien features,

although it didn't diminish the intensity of his stare. He had a way of looking at me as if he could see all the way into the depths of my soul.

"Szaro!"

Our heads jerked to the side to see Mandha approaching quickly.

"Brother?" Szaro asked when his sibling closed the distance with us.

"We must head out to the Chiswa Valley," Mandha said with a sliver of anger in his voice. "There is a pack of Flayers on a rampage there. We believe the Zamorian was luring beasts from this main pack which has ended up wandering further north"

Szaro emitted a low-pitched hiss filled with a slightly rattling sound. It was scary as fuck and yet there was something inherently sexy about it.

"Head out with the others," Szaro said. "I'll join you shortly."

Mandha nodded before turning around and moving at dizzying speed. Once again, it struck me how silent their movements were. For some reason, I'd always assumed their underside scales would make a grinding sound on the stone-paved ground.

"I don't want to hold you back," I said.

"You're not," Szaro replied in a gentle tone. "But the Chiswa Valley—named after the main species inhabiting it—is still in a fragile state. They are small, vulnerable creatures that are just now bouncing back from a bad infection that decimated their population. They cannot handle another blow so soon after their recovery."

"I can imagine," I said with a concerned frown.

"Once all of this is over, I will take you there," Szaro promised while looking over my shoulder.

I turned around to see Irco returning with an enthusiastic expression.

"I must leave my mate in your care," Szaro said as soon as the builder reached us. "She has many requirements for the dwelling as well. Give her whatever she desires. When you are done, inform Salha. She will see to Serena's other needs."

"Understood," Irco said with a deference that took me aback.

Szaro wasn't his tribe's leader but appeared to be their top hunter. Did that confer him some kind of status or upper hierarchy ranking? He certainly acted with a level of authority that the others followed.

"Thank you," Szaro responded before turning to me. "I will return in time for our bonding. It is a beautiful ritual. I hope you will enjoy it."

"See you later," I said with a smile, feeling awkward about the situation. I was no blushing bride buzzing with excitement at the thought of my impending nuptial. "Be careful out there."

"Of course, my mate," he replied with a smile.

I watched him hasten away, feeling oddly bereft. As intimidating as he was, my 'husband' exuded a soothing aura of strength and confidence. After he faded from view, I turned back to Irco and recoiled when I found him staring intently at me.

"Szaro has waited a long time to find the one he would call his mate," Irco said in a strange tone. "He has fought many battles and won many challenges to earn one of the most sought-after dwellings in Krada where he could build the most perfect nest for his *Ashina*… his goddess. He has high expectations, and I've been counting the days until the moment came when I would work on that masterpiece. Nothing is too much. If you can imagine it, I will find a way to build it. Challenge me, mate of the Great Hunter."

My stomach knotted upon hearing those words. If this were a marriage of love, I would be over the moon knowing my husband was giving me carte blanche to build my fairy tale home. Once more, guilt washed over me. It felt so unfair that I should stand in the way of his life-long dream and make a farce of it all. He deserved so much better.

I didn't want to make any major structural changes that might turn off the female he would hopefully mate after my departure. And yet, as per Kayog's instructions, I needed to play the game enough to convince the tribe that he and I were making a real go at this relationship.

"Well, that is a tall order," I said with a nervous laugh. "Before we discuss turning his dwelling into a castle, let's start with the basic necessities. We can look at sprucing up the rest of the house over the upcoming days and weeks."

"Of course, Serena," Irco said with a big grin. "Such endeavors take time and finesse. I look forward to our collaboration. Let's go see that cleansing room."

He led the way to their communal hygiene room, and we spent the next half hour discussing options, location, and sketching variations. Irco was a freaking genius. Each new sketch surpassed the previous one. He had a keen mind, an incredible imagination, and to top it all, he carefully listened to understand what I wanted instead of trying to sell me his preferences. No sooner had we agreed upon the design than he had four people going to work, first on the toilet—to my bladder's everlasting gratitude. I was particularly looking forward to the shower stall. Per the design, it would look out onto the hidden valley and possess a towel rack made out of a heating stone and a changing nook with a bench for me to put my clothes on so they wouldn't get soaked.

We then moved back to the house where we spent the next couple of hours discussing the basic essentials: a bed, some kind of kitchen, a living room, and above all, comfy seating for the terrace. I intended to enjoy the heck out of that place. To my delight, connectivity wasn't an issue here. I had not been certain, considering the Ordosians made no clear display of what technology they possessed. To my shock, Irco had already downloaded a vast library of human furniture that we spent a bit of time browsing through to identify the pieces I wanted made.

By the time we finished this first round, the workers had already built a functional enough toilet that I was at long last able to relieve my bladder before Irco handed me over to Salha. The female was beautiful, with shimmering green and blue scales that reminded me of a peacock's tail.

Unlike the males, who were all on the broader side and towered over me, Salha almost perfectly matched me in height and size. A more delicate version of the Ordosians' fins graced the outer side of her arms, and her hood, folded on the sides—like with most females—almost gave the illusion that she had straight blue hair framing her noble face. Two large bejeweled golden bracelets adorned her wrist, and a large necklace hung around her neck.

"Hello, mating-sister," Salha said in her slightly sibilant, yet oddly agreeable voice. "I hope everything went well with Irco?"

"Wonderfully! He's amazing. He's so patient and creative. I'm excited to see the finished product," I said in all sincerity.

"Good!" Salha said with a satisfied grin. "It is as it should be. Szaro will want the best for his mate."

"That's what he said," I replied, the sense of unease creeping back in.

Salha tilted her head to the side, giving me a strange look. "That doesn't seem to please you," she said.

My face heated, and I silently thanked God for my darker skin that hid my embarrassment. My sister-in-law was far too perceptive.

"It does please me that I should marry a male so generous," I said, carefully choosing my words. "I just feel guilty that he has spent so many years preparing all of this for his perfect mate but is instead stuck with me."

"He is not *stuck* with you," Salha said with conviction and a firmness that took me aback. "The Great Goddess Isshaya has sent you to us for a reason. Today, my son and I live because you came to us. And tonight, the Great Hunter of Krada will finally take a bonded mate. Do you have any idea how many of our females wanted that honor?"

"But he didn't *choose* me!" I exclaimed, guilt coming back at me with a vengeance. "He sacrificed himself out of duty because he feels indebted to me for saving you and your son."

Salha gave me an enigmatic smile as she shook her head. "No, sister of mine. Szaro never does anything he deems wrong out of obligation. If he didn't want you as a mate, he would have left the tribe and taken you to safety before he allowed any harm to come to you. He would have dealt with the diplomatic fallout afterwards."

My jaw dropped upon hearing those words. She smiled before giving the main room an assessing look. Salha slowly circled around the table, her slender fingers caressing the smooth, polished top.

"The first time Szaro saw this dwelling, he knew it would be his and that it would become the perfect nest for his *Ashina*," she said wistfully. "My mate's brother has a sense about things. Once he has decided he wants something, he will not stray from the path, no matter the cost or hardships to achieve his goal. The first time he saw you, his heart claimed you, even though his mind may not have known it."

I snorted in disbelief. "I highly doubt that. The first time we met, he looked at me like I was some sort of fascinating little insect."

"You are right about the fascination part," Salha said. "I saw his stance while he defended you before the Elders yesterday. After he left you in the detention room, he came to our dwelling, and I heard his words about you. The Temern didn't convince him to bond with you. Szaro had already decided to claim you as his mate last night. In his mind, he did so to save you, but I know my mating-brother. It is his heart that spoke. There's a reason none of our females found grace in his eyes."

"And what is that?" I asked, reeling.

"You are a Hunter, like him," Salha said matter-of-factly. "Ordosian females do not hunt or fight."

"Why? You're not allowed?" I asked, frowning.

Salha laughed. "Everyone is allowed to do what they want, as long as it doesn't threaten the safety of the tribe or of the world in our care," she said with an indulgent smile. "It is simply not in our nature. We are born nurturers and thinkers. We raise the young, head all scientific and medical efforts, and lead our tribes. Our males hunt, build, and protect both our tribes and the wilderness in our care."

"Right," I said. "I'm not much of a scientific head and have no desire to lead. But I do love to hunt and always pictured myself becoming a ranger in some national park."

"And now, you get to be a ranger alongside your mate, for an entire planet, with the most exotic creatures of our galaxy," Salha said smugly.

Put that way, it had a very sexy ring to it.

"I know you see it as punishment to have been forced to take this course of action for showing mercy to my son and me," Salha said in a gentle voice. "But this is fate. I've seen the way you look at Szaro. Ordosians may be strange to you in appearance, but you're still drawn to our Great Hunter. Do not overthink your situation, Serena. Let nature take its course. You are exactly where you are meant to be."

I shifted on my feet, feeling more troubled than I'd ever admit. I couldn't deny feeling a certain attraction towards Szaro. We were technically married now, and nobody was waiting for me back home. I *could* explore the possibilities of a relationship with him if I wanted to. But I couldn't think in those terms right now. All of this was still too fresh and too overwhelming.

"Let's see how things evolve," I said noncommittally.

"Let's," Salha replied. "Now, I will show you where to get food whenever you are hungry. I understand that besides meat, you also require fruits and vegetables?"

"Yes, that's correct," I said, following her out of the house. "Irco is going to build me a hot plate and an oven so that I can cook my meals, especially the meat."

"You cook everything?" Salha asked with a strange expression.

"Meat, yes," I said with a nod. "It is difficult for humans to digest raw meat. Not only is it harder for us to chew and digest, but we also get less nutrients from it *and* could get food poisoning from the bacteria some meat can contain."

"Hmmm, that would not be good," Salha said.

"Definitely *not* good," I replied with a chuckle.

"So how do you cook your meat?" she asked.

I explain to her the different methods of meat preparation, from braised, grilled, and roasted, to the spices and marinades, and side dishes. She stared at me in shock as I talked about the various courses of a meal, from appetizers to desserts, wine pairing, etc. The fact that we had different types of meals for specific times of the day also appeared to blow her mind.

"If you have to eat three times a day, just how much of your day do you devote to these meal preparations? The cooking process sounds complicated," Salha asked, flabbergasted, as we entered the building that I had mistaken for a greenhouse.

"It depends. Some meals can be prepared very quickly, while others take a lot of time," I said. "Breakfast can be done in a matter of minutes, unless you start going for the much fancier stuff. The same can be true of any other meal as long as you have everything handy in your fridge, and you're not making complicated recipes. But yes, preparing and eating food takes a notable part of the day. However, it is also an important bonding and social ritual for us."

"How so?" she asked, luring me to the back of this magnificent atrium where a number of small creatures were scurrying about while even stranger ones flew between the tall trees and thick foliage.

"We will often organize large dinners with family or friends. There's a lot of food involved that usually takes a few hours to prepare, and the meal itself can last a couple of hours or more while we talk and reminisce about things or tease each other."

Salha frowned, a troubled expression crossing her features. "How distraught would you be if you could no longer have those large family dinners?"

"I'm a bit of a loner. So, I wouldn't be distraught per se, but I can't deny that I would miss the occasional sitting down together to have a bite or a drink," I replied with a shrug. "I'm guessing from that question that Ordosians do not congregate to share meals?"

She shook her head and scrunched her face. "Eating is a chore that we like to expedite. But it's also a time of vulnerability for us."

She stopped to point at the fruit trees in the atrium.

"You can take any of the fruits directly from the trees and bushes here, but you can also come here at the back where we have gathered many of them in these containers and cooling units. Through the back door, you will find both our gardens and pens," Salha said before picking up an empty basket on the table then opening the door. "Harvest what you want and pick whatever creature you will want for your meat. We only ask that you do not pick anything bigger than you can consume. Although, in your case, we can cut up the meat and put it in a cooling unit for future meals."

I nodded looking at the crazy variety of vegetables, neatly labelled in the large garden.

"Why did you say that food is a chore and makes you vulnerable?" I asked.

"We swallow our food whole, usually still alive," Salha said casually. "It can take some time for it to go down, time during which we're pretty much useless, if not semi-lethargic. And then, depending on what we ate, especially in the case of a furry creature or one with horns, we will regurgitate those non-edible parts. It's not painful, but it's not exactly fun either. Like I said, just a chore. Which is why it's so great that we only have to deal with it once or twice a month as adults."

It took every ounce of my willpower to keep a neutral expression plastered on my face. I did *not* want to visualize them with their mouths widening to impossible sizes as they swallowed a rabbit whole, or their necks stretching beyond normal, or them puking out claws and horns like a cat threw out furballs. None of this evoked a sexy image.

"I see," I said in a small voice, which only appeared to amuse Salha, not fooled in the least.

The pens contained an impressive number of small creatures, some no bigger than a large mouse, and others closer to a little goat.

While Salha continued talking, I gathered a few vegetables and selected a kweelzy, a small creature that vaguely resembled a piglet. To my delight, one of the Ordosians who served as caretaker for some of the carnivorous animals in the atrium, butchered it for me. Although I could have done it myself, with my current limited equipment, I appreciated being spared the chore.

When I returned home, a cooling unit in my soon-to-be kitchen received my freshly acquired food, and Salha provided me with some basic comforts like cushions, glasses, and utensils. By the time she left me to go care for her young and prepare for my Ordosian wedding, my house was starting to take shape.

CHAPTER 7
SZARO

A thrill ran through me as we returned to the village. Despite the strangeness of our situation, I was excited to see my soon-to-be-bonded mate and see how she had begun to make our dwelling a home. The differences between us were proving far greater than I had first anticipated—at least from an anatomical standpoint—but it would take a lot more to deter me from my goal.

A grin tugged at my lips as I approached my dwelling to find Irco setting up a cooking area alongside the left wall, right outside.

"There you are!" Irco said warmly. "I'm making good progress."

"So I see," I replied.

"I partially owe the Temern for that," the builder confessed.

"Oh?"

"He sent a hot plate and a cooking oven with an adaptor for our power sources," Irco continued. "Without that, it would have taken us a couple of weeks at least to build one from scratch for your mate."

Although pleased by this quick solution, I frowned. “You asked Kayog for equipment?”

Irco laughed. “No, Great Hunter. Kayog sent it, along with various things your mate might require, like blankets, towels, cooking pots, and other things. He called it a wedding gift on behalf of the UPO,” he explained.

“Ah... very well, then,” I said, relieved. “But why are you building this outside?”

“Serena and I agreed that, with the dwelling being inside a cave, despite the good ventilation, it is better to keep the cooking outside,” Irco replied. “Since we have warm weather throughout the year, it will not be a problem for her. However, I will build a roof and half walls so that she can still use it when it rains. I’m going to add a couple of counters here and here.”

“Can you add a sink?” I asked.

“Yes,” Irco said, pursing his lips. “But I will have to pierce through the wall to connect it to the one inside.”

“Do it. I want the best for my mate,” I said firmly. “And her hygiene needs?”

“The shower is already set up. The ‘toilet’ is functional, but it’s still a work in progress. In truth, I wanted to discuss this with you before we finished,” Irco said sheepishly.

“What’s wrong?” I asked, immediately concerned.

“There’s nothing wrong, but your mate is quite modest in her requests,” Irco said, shifting uneasily. “Based on what she explained to me, humans use their toilets multiple times in a day, unlike us who only go once a week or so.”

“That is correct,” I said.

“Well, she mentions that they sometimes have to go during the night,” Irco continued. “It seems quite inconvenient for your female to have to leave your dwelling in the middle of the night to go to the cleansing area just to use the toilet. Our nights can be chilly, and humans have no proper night vision like we do.”

I stiffened, my eyes widening in understanding. “Excellent

observation, Irco," I said, berating myself for not having thought of it myself. "It would be better to have a toilet directly inside our dwelling, and a shower as well while we are at it."

"Agreed," Irco said, perking up. "But your mate immediately dismissed the idea when I suggested it. She felt it was too much work when we already had something functional, and that as a new member of our tribe, she should adapt to our ways."

While her diplomatic answer to Irco pleased me, I knew the real reason behind her refusal. Serena was trying to keep the changes to our dwelling to a minimum so it wouldn't be too hard to undo once she left. Even that outdoor kitchen would be easily dismantled without leaving a single trace of its existence should that day come.

I will see that it never does.

"An admirable sentiment," I said nonchalantly, "but I will not have my mate traipsing around outside at night because I failed to provide her with all the proper comforts required for her species. You will build a proper hygiene room for my mate in the house. She loves the view onto the hidden valley. Can it be built at the back of the dwelling with a large window looking out?"

"Yes, Szaro," Irco said, his voice bubbling with excitement. "It will be a little tricky, but it can definitely be done. We browsed images of human hygiene rooms. In addition to the shower and the waste seat, many contained large tubs that fill with water in which humans can relax or bathe. There was this one model that your mate really liked," he said, flipping through the images of his tablet to show me. "I can recreate something close to this in one of your back rooms. And Terya can carve ornaments on the walls similar to this."

A slow grin stretched my lips. "Do it. And have her embed glowstones in the bigger circles in the pattern," I added.

"Oh, yes! That will be a nice touch!" Irco said approvingly. "I will tell Terya."

"I will go see my mate now and prepare for our bonding. I'll see you later," I said.

"See you soon, Great Hunter," Irco replied as I turned to enter my dwelling.

Silence greeted me. For a moment, I wondered if she was out, but Irco would have told me as much. Was she sleeping? I immediately dismissed that idea. Humans were diurnal beings like us. I flicked my tongue, tasting the air for traces of Serena.

The terrace.

Of course, I should have known. It had greatly fascinated her. I headed straight to the back of the dwelling and pushed the door, which opened quietly onto the balcony. The vision that awaited me took my breath away.

Standing with her back to me, facing the stunning view of the valley, Serena was performing strange movements on top of a black mat, holding weird, stretched poses for a few moments before switching to another. For the first time, I got to see the golden beauty of her exposed brown skin. Barefoot, my mate was wearing nothing but a skin-tight lower garment from her waist to the middle of her thighs—making her legs look infinite—and a top without arms that only covered her breasts.

I observed her quietly, mesmerized by the grace of her movements, the impossible poses she executed, the undeniable strength some of them required, and her incredible sense of balance to maintain them. But even more fascinating were the things she could do with her legs. I don't know how long I stayed there, transfixed by my mate. She took on this weird pose, leaning on her forearms, which rested flat on the mat, her head lifted to look straight ahead with her body raised over her, her pointed feet almost dangling in front of her face. If she pushed them any further, her body would form a proper O.

She must have sensed my presence at last because her head jerked down, and Serena looked behind her between her arms supporting her body. My mate's eyes widened in surprise, and her body tipped forward. She yelped as she fell and ended up lying on her back.

"Serena!" I shouted, rushing to her side.

From the way she'd fallen, she could have broken her arms. Even as I lowered myself next to her, she sat up, rolling her shoulders while grimacing.

"Are you all right?" I asked, worry knotting my inside.

"Yeah, I'm fine," she said, giving me a reassuring smile. "You startled me, that's all. I was in the zone and didn't hear you come in."

"I'm sorry. I should have announced my arrival," I said, still checking for any signs she'd been injured. "I was just fascinated by what you were doing. What was that?"

"It's called yoga," Serena explained. "It's a great way to meditate, exercise, and to work on your strength and flexibility."

"It is quite amazing. I didn't think humans could move that way," I said, genuinely impressed.

"You have no idea all the ways I can move," Serena said smugly, further piquing my curiosity. "I'll have to show you sometime."

"I'm looking forward to it," I said with a grin. "I just wanted to let you know that I have returned."

"How did the hunt go?" Serena asked with a sincere curiosity that made me feel warm inside.

"It went well. Thankfully, we arrived early enough to prevent any serious damage to the Chiswa population. But there are other herds roaming close to the forbidden areas to the northwest. Our scouts are monitoring their progress to see whether we will need to intervene or not."

"I'm glad to hear you were able to contain it. No one's injured, I hope?" she asked, while starting to get up.

I instinctively extended a hand to help her. She didn't need it and appeared stunned by the gesture. Still, she accepted my assistance with a smile. A sudden heat coursed through me at the softness of her hand in mine and the silkiness of her skin. I'd never touched her before, or any other human for that matter. I had not expected this. When she gently pulled out of my grasp, I almost reached for her again. I swallowed hard and flicked my tongue to get another taste of her for lack of her touch. My fingers burned with the need to further explore the delicate wonder that was my mate, but she wasn't ready to do any such things with me… yet.

"No one's injured," I confirmed. "AND 36 new Flayers have been added to your score in the Hunt," I continued with a smug smile.

"WHAT?!" Serena exclaimed, shock plastered all over her face.

"You are Ordosian now and my mate. The tribe's kills are your kills. I claimed all of them for you," I said proudly.

"But… Why would you do that? I mean, don't get me wrong, that's amazing! But why did you?" Serena asked, looking genuinely confused. "I figured you'd be furious with everything related to the hunt."

"The hunt has its upsides and downsides," I said with a shrug. "But you are my mate. It is my duty to see to your present and future welfare. Whatever fate and the Goddess may have planned for us, I want all of your needs well-taken care of. These extra credits will help ensure your comfort, whether to resume your travels or to purchase foreign goods and have them delivered here."

"You're really sweet and thoughtful," Serena said, looking at me with an expression I could not identify.

"With you only," I said teasingly to hide my embarrassment. "But now, we must prepare for our bonding ceremony," I added in a gentle voice. "It will start within the hour."

"Oh!" she said, an uncertain look descending on her features. "What… what should I do? What should I wear?"

"We must shower, so that we come to each other cleansed of

any burden of our past," I explained. "Females usually come bare, as they bring wisdom, nurturing, and life to the union, all of which are contained within themselves. It is the male who adorns himself to display his strength and ability to provide for his dwelling. As your species does not go around bare, you may wear what you wish."

"Okay, I can do that," she said, licking her lips nervously. "Is there anything specific that I'm expected to do during the ceremony?"

"Normally, there would be," I replied gently, "but it would be too complex for you to learn, and I doubt your anatomy would allow you to perform it as it would require a tail and greater physical strength than you possess. It has already been discussed with the Elders, and they agreed with how we will proceed," I added quickly when she seemed on the verge of panic. "You will sit and observe the ritual, then you will join me. We will embrace and kiss under the blessing of the Elders. You only have to stand there and hold me, I will take care of everything. It won't be long, so you shouldn't be too indisposed."

"Oh, that's fine," she replied with a nervous laugh. "I can hold you for however long it takes. I just don't want to make a fool of myself or embarrass you."

"You won't," I said in a reassuring tone. "Come, let us go shower. Take the clothes you intend to wear as you will not return here. Salha will take you directly from the cleansing room to the Great Circle."

"Salha? Where will you be?" she asked, confused.

"I will return here to adorn myself," I said with a grin.

"Riiight, I forgot that. All right then," Serena said with a frown, her face taking on a pensive expression.

I suspected she was mentally reviewing what clothes she had in order to pick something appropriate. She headed to our rest room, which I hadn't seen since my return. To my delight, a large human-style bed had been set up next to my heating plate.

Irco had brought in a dresser for Serena, as well as a rack on which some of her outfits hung. Later, he would build a proper space for her to put those clothes. But right now, seeing my previously empty space becoming crowded with my mate's belongings and filling up with her scent reawakened that warm feeling in my chest.

"I'm afraid I don't have a white dress, as is our tradition," Serena said sheepishly. "But I hope this little black dress will be acceptable."

"Human clothes make little sense to me," I said in an apologetic tone. "All that matters is that you are happy and comfortable with the ones you will wear tonight."

"I love that dress," she said with a timid smile. "It makes me look good… I think."

"Then the little black dress it is," I said, finding her expression adorable. "Let us go, my mate."

As we made our way to the cleansing area, we passed a number of my people, many of them already adorned for the celebration. Theirs adornments were simple and muted so that I could shine in their midst. While Serena appeared to grow more nervous, excitement bubbled within me. It was irrational. I should be as worried as my female but, as illogical as it was, this felt right.

I parted ways with Serena when we entered and made my way towards Mandha and Raskier, who awaited me with scrubbing stones. A short distance from us, near the window overlooking the hidden valley, Salha was waiting for my mate next to her newly built enclosed shower.

My tribe mates were timid at first, uncertain of my frame of mind under the circumstances. But when they saw my cheery mood, both males relaxed and teased me with the traditional pre-bonding raunchy comments while washing my tail and back. At the same time, I polished my front, face and arms with the stones.

We finished before Serena was done. A good thing, as it would give me more time to properly adorn myself. Mandha came with me back to my dwelling, further assisting me as I put on my necklace made from the polished teeth of the most vicious beasts I'd defeated to display my strength, a pair of bracers made of precious metals and gems to display my ability to provide, and upper arm rings—right below my shoulders, but just above my fins—that I crafted myself to showcase not only my skills but also my rank and achievements. I then moved to my armory to select my most exquisite battle staff, which could be split to turn into a pair of vicious blades. Along with Raskier, Mandha would perform the warrior's dance with me tonight as I had done for him on his bonding night.

We exited my dwelling and made our way to the Great Circle where my destiny awaited.

CHAPTER 8
SERENA

I didn't get why I felt so nervous as Salha led me to the massive amphitheater they called the Great Circle. This wasn't going to be a true wedding, just the formality to secure my safe stay with the tribe for the next few months. Still, I felt jitters. But those worries quickly took a backseat as I feasted my eyes on the mesmerizing sight before me.

As they couldn't comfortably navigate stairs, the 'seating' area was basically an incline, not so steep as to make it uncomfortable, but just enough that people in the back were higher than those in the front and could still have a clear view of what was happening on the huge circular platform at the bottom. Large braziers surrounded the circle, and a fascinating pale blue flame burned within them. It almost looked like a magical flame.

Standing around the edges of the circle, a dozen Ordosian females held long ribbons of the same pale-blue color as the flames. In the encroaching darkness of early nightfall, a slight glow radiated around them. They reminded me of the ribbons from my old days as a rhythmic gymnast. Behind them, on an elevated dais, the three Elders towered over the area. And beyond, to complete this magnificent tableau, the river trickled down in a happy flow.

A hush descended over the tribe assembled for the event as Salha led me to the cushioned, U-shaped stool at the edge of the circle, right where the 'seating' area ended. She made me remove my shoes before entering it. As soon as I was settled, Salha went to join the twelve females in the center. One of them extended a pair of ribbons to my sister-in-law, who slipped her hands into a sort of glove at the end of each.

My jaw dropped when all of the females lifted the tips of their tails and their scales parted, revealing whitish bulbs that seemed to swell. From where I sat, it made the tips of their tail look vaguely like lilies of the valley. Salha emitted a long, sustained cry that startled me. It wasn't a shout or scream, but more like a call to gather. As soon as she stopped, the females began rattling their tails in almost perfect sync, the sound akin to a strong wind rustling through the leaves of a tree. Seconds later, they started singing in a manner similar to the Inuit Throat-Singers. The crowd soon responded to their haunting chant by interjecting throaty sounds at specific moments, their own tail rattles also joining the fray.

Mesmerized, I stared in awe as the females began to sway from side to side in an incredibly sensual motion. Salha made that calling sound again before raising her arms and moving around in a tight circle, all while waving her ribbons. The other females imitated her for a few seconds, then launched into an enchanting choreography. They appeared to glide around the circle, ribbons swirling and twirling around them, looking almost like light waves dancing in the air in the growing darkness.

Salha, still in the center of the circle, was performing what could have passed for the Ordosian version of belly dancing. In that instant, I realized that she was performing on my behalf the dance that I should have done. While a part of me was grateful for them sparing me from this, another part felt that, as this was my wedding, I should have performed my own version of a dance instead.

But the sound of drums being struck once every two seconds had my head jerk left then right. Four males slithered from the sides, beating their drums in perfect sync as they went to take their position at the edge of the circle.

A war cry rose in the distance. I recognized the voice as belonging to Szaro. A most pleasant shiver of anticipation ran through me. Two voices echoed his war cry, their tone menacing. As if in direct response, the four males by the circle began beating their drums in a martial fashion. The females moved to the edges, swaying from side to side while still waving their ribbons. Salha came to stand by my side.

My breath caught in my throat as I watched Szaro enter the circle with a savage expression on his face, the badass battle staff I'd admired in his armory held firmly in his hand. The two males I had yet to see continued to shout war cries from the sides while Szaro began performing a dance of his own, waving his staff around with the dexterity of a marching band drum major, swirling it around his body and neck, tossing it into the air and catching it flawlessly, the whole time flexing his muscles, stretching his hood to make himself look even more fearsome and imposing, and swaying in a way that had me hot and bothered in no time.

He moved closer to me and struck his staff on the ground. The movement of his hips made his abdominal muscles ripple, causing my mouth to water. He rattled the tip of his tail next to my ear, and the sound resonated deep in my core.

My nipples instantly hardened, and wetness pooled between my thighs. Szaro flicked his tongue, and his slitted pupils widened. A hungry look descended over his features, making me squirm in my seat.

Just as I was about to give in to the burning urge to reach out and touch him, Szaro pulled away. Mandha and Raskier rushed into the circle, each armed with a weapon. They immediately attacked him in a battle worthy of the most epic martial arts choreography. I couldn't tell if it was a real fight or not, but it had me at the edge of my seat. It also turned me on far more than I wanted to admit to myself.

When Szaro split his staff in two, revealing vicious blades at the tips of each half to simultaneously fight his two opponents, I got so caught up in the moment that I jumped to my feet and started shouting encouragement. Salha's laughter next to me snapped me out of my daze. Her knowing smile and approving gaze made me blush. But as the beat of the drums and the throaty chants of the females and of the crowd reached a crescendo, everything suddenly stopped. Silence descended over the circle. Mandha and Raskier slithered backwards, heads bowed, hoods folded, and arms spread wide with their weapons lowered in a gesture of defeat.

Szaro moved to the center of the circle and emitted a victorious war cry to which everyone responded with the rattling of their tails. That sound didn't affect me like Szaro's had when he'd done it next to my ear. He reattached the two halves of his staff into a single weapon, placed it on the ground next to him and extended both hands towards me. Salha led me to him. He drew me into his embrace, and I wrapped my arms around him.

Fuck me sideways!! My knees turned to jelly at the hard feel of his chest against mine. I'd expected his scales to be hard and to scrape my skin, but they were smooth to the touch. He towered over me by a good head—his hood spread wide, blocking out the full moon behind him. His pupils widened as his gaze bore into mine, hypnotizing me. Szaro's tail wrapped around us twice, drawing me even more closely to him, and yet still leaving enough length for the tip to rise next to my ear and rattle. A moan escaped me as a bolt of lust exploded in the pit of my stomach.

A fierce smile stretched his lips, baring his fangs that

appeared longer than ever. My breath caught in my throat as he leaned forward, a rumbling sound vibrating from his chest. My fingers dug into his muscular back, expecting the impending sting from his fangs sinking into my flesh, but he merely rubbed his cheek against mine on one side and then on the other, marking me with his scent. The gentle scraping of the scales alongside his jaw on my skin resonated directly in my core. His hold tightened as I moaned again, the sustained rattling of his tail working like the most potent of aphrodisiacs.

When he straightened to look at me, a flash of light blue at the edge of my vision made me realize the females had resumed their dance, swirling their ribbons around us. I felt some of them brush against my arms and back, but they didn't matter to me: Szaro did. His strong hand slid up my spine to cup my nape moments before he claimed my mouth. Liquid fire poured through my veins. It wasn't the chaste kiss from our human wedding. This was possessive, dominant, and passionate.

Just as I was melting in his arms, he broke the kiss, his lips tracing a burning trail along my jawline and down my neck. A soft gasp escaped me, turning into a moan when the prickling sensation of his fangs piercing the fleshy part of my shoulder was soon followed by an overall sense of well-being due to whatever he'd just injected me with.

Szaro straightened as silence once more surrounded us. Feeling a little disoriented, I noticed the females had moved to the side while the three Elders had descended from the dais. They surrounded us, all three of them holding hands to form a circle around us. They began speaking in Ordosian, reciting something in one voice. I had no idea what they said but could guess it was some sort of blessing. Szaro smiled with a tenderness that turned me upside down before pressing his forehead to mine.

We remained like this while the Elders continued to speak, the tribe chorusing a single word from time to time. Finally,

Elder Krathi spoke alone. Szaro responded in their language, startling me.

"Serena, do you freely accept Szaro Kota as your life mate?" Elder Krathi asked in Universal this time.

"I do," I responded.

"Serena Bello, Szaro Kota, you are bonded for life before the Goddess Isshaya and the people of Krada. May your union be happy, fertile, and endless in years," Elder Krathi said in a solemn voice.

The sound of the entire tribe rattling their tails was like a tidal wave, sending a shiver down my spine. The Elders released their hands and moved away from us, breaking the circle. Szaro's hold around me tightened ever so slightly. Lifting his forehead from mine, he kissed my lips one more time, then my forehead before releasing me with obvious reluctance. Although I couldn't swear it, my gut told me these last two kisses had not been part of the ceremony. To my total dismay, I wished he hadn't stopped.

The next hour or so went by in a daze as the tribe descended from the 'seating' area of the amphitheater to congratulate us. Szaro introduced me to each tribe member, their names flying right out of my mind within seconds, some of them striking brief conversations with us, then slowly scattering. Eventually, most of the tribe had moved away, leaving only Salha, her mate, and her child. To my shock, she pulled me into her embrace.

"Welcome to the family, my sister," she said affectionately before releasing me.

"Welcome to the family," Mandha repeated, bowing his head as Salha let go of me.

"Welcome to the family," Eicu said with his young, high-pitched voice, standing half-hidden behind his father.

"Thank you," I said, feeling both touched and like an impostor.

"Enjoy the moment, my sister," Salha said, while handing me

back my shoes. "Remember that you are right where you are meant to be."

With these words, she waved us goodbye and left with her family.

"Ready to go home, my mate?" Szaro asked, his voice sounding deeper than before.

Suddenly intimidated, I nodded, unable to speak a word. He placed his hand on the small of my back to give me a nudge forward. I barely repressed a shiver, feeling instantly bereft by the brevity of his touch. As we made our way back to our house, I realized how much Szaro had to slow his natural speed to adjust to the pace of my normal human walk. Thankfully, it didn't seem to faze him.

"Do you require sustenance?" he asked in a solicitous fashion as soon as we entered our dwelling.

I shook my head, touched by his attention. "No," I said with a smile. "I ate right before you arrived. I'm fine until morning."

"Very well," he said, looking as uncertain as I felt.

"It was a beautiful ceremony," I said with sincerity. "You all dance amazingly well. It was impressive, especially you battling those two males."

Szaro straightened proudly, a wide grin stretching his lips. "I am glad it pleased you."

An awkward silence settled between us as we both looked for something to say. I tried to come up with something, but my stupid, lust-filled brain kept turning back to the feel of his hard body wrapped around me and his lips pressing against mine. How could I be such a horn ball for a male I probably wasn't even compatible with?

"I guess I should get ready for bed," I said nervously. "It's been a long and eventful day."

"Of course," Szaro said.

I headed to our bedroom while Szaro went to his armory to put away his weapon. Just as I was closing the drawer of my dresser after retrieving one of my nightgowns, the door opened on Szaro. My head jerked towards him as he glided in while removing one of his armbands. He stopped dead in his tracks when he noticed the expression on my face.

"Is something wrong, my mate?" he asked with a sliver of worry.

I chewed my bottom lip, feeling even more awkward and silly for being so self-conscious. As my husband, he was entitled to see me naked. But this was no traditional wedding.

And I am far too eager for a repeat after that kiss.

"Everything is fine. It's just…" I searched for the words to explain that I was just being a dumb prude when his gaze settled on the garment clutched in my hands.

His face lit up with understanding. "Privacy," he whispered under his breath. "Humans do not undress in front of others, except their mate. You will have privacy until you feel ready to welcome me as a mate. I will wait outside. Let me know when it is fine for me to return."

"No! You don't have to do that!" I exclaimed, feeling like a total shit. "I'm being silly."

"No, my mate. You have been thrown into a situation you weren't ready for," he said gently. "The day you bare yourself in my presence, it will be because you *want* to, not because you feel you *have* to. I will not have you ever be uncomfortable because of me. I will be outside."

He turned around and exited the room, closing the door behind him. Even though there had been no condemnation in his eyes, and although I doubted neither the sincerity of his words nor the sentiment that fueled them, I still felt guilty and conflicted. Nevertheless, I made quick work of stripping out of my second skin of a little black dress to put on my midnight blue silk negligée.

"You can come in," I called out while hanging my dress on my temporary clothes rack.

Szaro returned, his gaze roaming over me like a gentle caress. It did funny things to me, and I was baffled to realize that, despite my human body, my husband appeared to genuinely be attracted to me. When Salha had gone on about his fascination with me, I thought she'd been overhyping it to help things along between us.

"This is a beautiful color and fabric on you," Szaro said simply before turning to his dresser.

"Thank you," I said, flattered. "It's my favorite color."

I climbed into my bed, my gaze locked on him as he carefully removed his adornments and put them back inside his dresser.

"You're staring," he said without turning to look at me.

I stiffened. "How do you know?"

Like king cobras, the Ordosians had two patterns at the back of their hood that looked like eyes.

"I can feel it," he replied, matter-of-factly, as he turned to face me.

"Sorry," I mumbled, scrunching my face.

"Why sorry? I am your mate. You have the right to look and touch all you like," he said with a shrug. "I have no secrets from you. It is my duty to sate your curiosity about me or my species as a whole."

I sat up in my bed and crossed my legs under me, my blanket covering any naughty bits my short skirt might have revealed. I gave him an assessing look, my gaze slowly roaming over him. His lips twitched with amusement, and he spread his arms wide before doing a slow 360.

I snorted. "Someone is showing off," I said teasingly.

"It's only showing off if the watchers like what they see," he deadpanned. "Should I presume that my appearance, strange though it is to a human, doesn't displease you?"

I chuckled, wondering if he was fishing for compliments. "I'll admit that, as much as I found you intimidating the first time we met, you're growing on me. You're not hard on the eyes—hood, scales, tail, and all."

It was his turn to chuckle. "You flatter me, my mate," he said, bowing his head. "I think your face is enchanting, and your skin is a wonder, both in its unique golden color and incredible softness. Legs are still a mystery to me, but what you can do with yours fascinates me beyond words. What you did on the terrace earlier, I could have watched you for hours. You are more than not hard on the eyes, my mate, you are a pleasure to gaze upon."

I stared at him speechless for a moment. "Wow… You sure know how to speak to a woman," I said, beyond moved.

"I take that as being positive?" he asked hesitantly.

I nodded. "Most definitely."

He grinned, his shoulders relaxing. He looked so different from the scary hunter that I had first met by the border.

"But ask away. I'm sure there are things you want to know about me," Szaro insisted.

He wrapped his tail neatly and lowered himself upon it in what I considered his sitting position. I smiled gratefully as it put him at eye-level with me sitting on my bed instead of having to strain my neck to look up at him.

"Actually, I do have a number of questions," I admitted sheepishly. "Please do not hesitate to tell me if they are rude or make you uncomfortable. I do not want to offend you."

"I won't be. Ask away. I am curious to know what kind of things about us intrigue you."

I cleared my throat, shifted on my bed, then went for it. "Do you… do you molt?"

Szaro burst out laughing. It was powerful, deep, and sexy, with the same subtle vibrating sound that always accompanied the Ordosians' speech.

"We do," he said with a nod. "And it's downright insufferable. The itchiness is enough to drive one to madness. You will get to witness me going insane in two or three weeks."

I couldn't help but laugh at his dejected expression. "Is it really that bad?" I asked in a commiserating voice.

"It is," he replied grumpily. "You just want to rip it off, but you can't, or you might end up tearing off some of the new scales. At least, at my age, we only molt once or twice a year. For younglings, it's once a month." He frowned before casting a playfully baleful glance my way. "You will probably die of laughter watching me for ten days as I rub myself over every rough surface I encounter to help loosen the old skin."

I chuckled again at the visual of Szaro scratching against a rock or a tree like a big bear with an itch.

"And does it come off in a single piece like most snakes?" I asked.

He shook his head. "No. The old skin on the arms tends to fall off first. You'd think the one around our tail would be first since it's constantly grinding on the ground, but no. Our hood and back are second. And then the torso and the tail come off in a single piece. Then our scales are all beautiful and shiny, and we don't feel so confined anymore in a skin that's too tight to contain us."

"That must feel good," I said.

"Very! Until then, I apologize in advance for how irritable I might get during that time," he added with a guilty face. "Drinking a lot of water and soaking in the river helps alleviate some of the symptoms."

"Then I guess we'll be swimming a lot in two weeks," I said teasingly.

"Indeed. What else do you want to know about me?"

"Hmm… You don't have ears, or at least none that are visible. How do you hear what I say?" I asked.

"We do not have external ears, but we have inner ones. Sound travels from our skin to our jaw muscles, to the quadrate bone next to our ear bone, and from there, the sound waves enter our inner ear."

"Nifty," I said, staring at the spot under his hood where external ears would have been on a human, and wondering what hearing that way might sound like.

"What else?"

I pursed my lips, holding back the question I really wanted to ask, and choosing to ease into the topic with a different question first.

"I was surprised to find out that Ordosians kiss," I said carefully. "It shouldn't have been one, considering you have lips identical to ours. But do you kiss with your tongues, too?"

"We do," he said with a naughty grin that had me squirming.

"But… don't you use it to smell?" I argued.

"We do that as well," he conceded. "Our tongue is even more sensitive to smell than our noses. It reveals many things, from distance, to gender, to health status, pregnancy, fear, and *arousal*, to name a few. It is quite a powerful tool."

My cheeks burned with embarrassment. The way he'd emphasized the word *arousal* made it clear he'd caught my scent on at least one of the many times he'd gotten me hot and bothered.

"I see," I said, losing my nerve to continue with my other question.

He narrowed his eyes at me, his face taking on a disturbing intensity.

"Go on, Serena. Ask me," Szaro suddenly said, his gaze darkening and his voice dropping almost an octave. "You've been wondering from the first time you laid eyes on me, and even more so once Kayog informed you that we were to bond to save your life. Ask me."

"If you know what I'm curious about, why don't you just tell me?" I challenged, scrunching my face with embarrassment.

"Because I want you to ask me," he said in an oddly commanding voice.

"Fine," I said in a slightly clipped tone. "Do you have hemipenes like most snakes and lizards?"

A slow grin stretched his lips, making my stomach flutter. There was something sexual about it that promised plenty of wicked times.

"No, my mate, there's no need for two penises," he said in a rumbling tone. "Snakes only use one at a time anyway. So, us having two would be pointless."

That revelation pleased me far too much. I licked my lips nervously and summoned all my courage to ask the next question.

"Snake penises have a few spikes on them. How about you guys?" I asked, shocked by my own boldness.

"A few?" Szaro repeated as if I'd said something offensive. "We don't have a few. Our penises are covered with them."

My jaw dropped, and my shoulders fell, shock and bitter disappointment warring within me. I shouldn't be so bummed out. His words only confirmed what I'd known all along: we weren't compatible. It still sucked. For a moment during our ceremony, while he held me in his arms, I actually wondered if I could give this a real chance…

Szaro burst out laughing at my crestfallen expression. "You have no idea how much it pleases me that you should be so disappointed. You and I are compatible. They are spikes, not thorns," he explained. "They are not sharp and rigid. Their tips are rounded, and they have just the right firmness to enhance a female's pleasure. And when I am aroused, I can make them pulsate for even greater sensations."

I gaped at him, speechless, unsure how to react or what to think. "Are you serious?" I asked at last, shocked that those would be the words to come out of my mouth.

"Very serious. Do you want to see?" he asked, matter-of-factly.

My brain froze for a second as I stared at him in disbelief. "Did you just offer to show me your dick?"

"If by 'dick' you mean penis, then yes. My body is yours," Szaro said with a shrug. "I have nothing to hide from you. I'm merely offering to show. I'm not trying to seduce you."

I chewed my bottom lip. My curiosity was beyond sky high. "All right, yes. I'd really like to see what you guys are packing down there," I said, my face burning.

The triumphant smile on Szaro's face made me wonder for a moment if it had been a mistake. But any such thoughts fled my mind as the scales a short distance below his navel—where a man's crotch would be—parted to reveal a seam from whence a thick, lubricated shaft emerged. My husband had not been kidding when he said his shaft was covered in spikes. However, now that I could see them, their rounded tips indeed erased any fear I initially felt. They weren't thorns or claw-like monstrosities that would tear me to shreds. Instead, I found myself imagining what it would feel like.

"See?" Szaro said with a grin. "It's not that threatening, is it?"

I shook my head, although my eyes remained locked on his shaft.

"What are you doing?" I exclaimed as he began to slowly stroke himself.

"Showing you how I can control them once I am aroused," he said, nonchalantly.

The wretch was taunting me—enjoying my embarrassment. And yet, I watched with fascination as his hand moved along his length a few more times.

"No way!" I exclaimed when, moments later, he stopped stroking himself, holding his shaft at the base so that I could see what was happening.

His spikes extruded a little further, and the head of his cock widened for a few seconds before returning to their normal sizes. He repeated the motion a few times, his gaze heavy on me.

"We resorb going in, and distend going out," he explained.

The dull throbbing between my thighs made me wish I could slip my hand under my skirt and take care of business. My face must have shown how hot and bothered he was getting me because Szaro flicked his tongue a couple of times in my direction.

"Don't do that," I said, scrunching my face to hide my embarrassment.

"Don't do what?" Szaro asked with the most fake innocent look on his face. "Taste the scent of your arousal?"

"Yes," I hissed.

"Why wouldn't I? It is divine, and it is my reward to reap," he said, smugly. "There is nothing wrong with being aroused by your mate, Serena. Quite the contrary… The sooner you let go of your inhibitions and fears, the sooner we can truly begin our life together."

He released his cock and retracted it inside his body, his scales closing seamlessly. I forced a neutral expression on my face to hide how much I wished it was still out and that he would use it on me.

"One thing I can promise you, my Serena, is that once you've been with an Ordosian, you'll have no more use for human men," he whispered in a purring tone that messed me up inside.

I gasped in disbelief at such an outrageous boast.

"Sweet dreams, my mate," Szaro said before I could respond. "May they be filled with pleasant thoughts of you and me."

And with that, he moved to his heated plate, wrapped his long tail into a round cushion before resting on top of it. I stared at him a few seconds longer, feeling cheated. Fighting back a frustrated groan, I lay down on my bed, turned off the light, and had many wet dreams about us.

CHAPTER 9
SZARO

I stirred yet again from what had been the most restless of nights. My gaze immediately landed on the sleeping form of my mate, so close to me yet out of reach. The scent of her arousal once more permeated the room. I ached to extrude and claim what our bonding entitled me to and what my mate also desired, despite her resistance. But I reined in the urge. I was the greatest Hunter of my tribe, and I loved a good chase. None was more worthy than this one. As much as she denied it, my prey was already caught. I just needed to be patient until she willingly surrendered.

And she would.

I had expected to fight a more arduous battle to change the way she looked at me and find grace in her eyes. It pleased me tremendously that she, too, was feeling the natural chemistry that existed between us. And last night, during the ceremony, when I held her in my arms, we connected on a deep level that even she couldn't deny. In that instant, my concerns that Serena would leave me at the end of our six-month trial evaporated. I would conquer her heart.

Even now, as much as her scent tortured me, as it had all

night, I couldn't help the smug grin that tugged at my lips. I'd give anything for a peek into whatever dreams were fanning her passion right now. I knew, at a visceral level, that it featured us.

Keep dreaming of us, my mate. Soon, I will make your fantasies a reality.

As sleep continues to evade me, I retrieved my tablet, which I rarely made use of, and resumed reading about a human's day-to-day life. My mate's species was very social, something Ordosians were not. We came together for specific things like last night's bonding, the occasional performance from our artistically oriented tribe members, for a vote, a ruling, or a sentencing, and for training or hunting.

Humans grouped with non-relatives all the time, just to spend time together. Some of it made little sense, like going to big shopping centers for hours, often with no intent whatsoever of buying anything. It constituted a massive waste of time and energy, but apparently served an important role as a bonding mechanism among peers or friends. We didn't have such centers here, so dwelling on that part served no purpose.

My biggest concern was for the other forms of social grouping. The majority appeared to revolve around food and drinks. Humans invited each other to their respective dwellings to share big meals, or they went to places that specialized in serving food to patrons, or they went to places where they could dance with each other and also share alcoholic beverages. We had none of that.

How essential is that for her?

My mate's nutritional needs were another major source of worry for me. My mind reeled with the variety of foods, spices, and beverages they consumed. For fruits, meats, and vegetables, we could find acceptable equivalents here. The challenge would be all the other things we didn't produce as none of us had any use for them, from cooking oils, to flour, to baking ingredients, and that black seed powder called coffee humans seemed so addicted to. We didn't even have olives, wheat, or coffee beans on Trangor. I would need to speak with Kayog to see by what means some of the non-perishable goods not obtainable here could be sent to us from off-world.

I will not allow this to be the reason she leaves me or feels miserable living here.

Still, I would ask our botanists to cross-reference our available fruits, vegetables, and grains to find their equivalent in the human diet. By the time I stopped that research, the sun was already rising over Krada. I carefully rose from my heated plate and quietly exited our room so as not to wake my mate. I headed to the atrium to gather and wash some fruits and filled a bowl with a variety of nuts to give her some protein.

To my delight, I ran into Hijara, one of the caretakers of the animals in the atrium and the hidden valley. She was often up early to make sure the weak and wounded creatures in either of these sanctuaries were properly fed. I discussed with her the basic components of one of the standard human breakfasts. Within minutes, she provided me with three different types of eggs, and cut a few thin slices of two different meats from one of the cooling units.

"Ask your mate to try those," Hijara said. "They have very different tastes. Hopefully, one will be close to the flavors of her homeworld."

"Thank you, Hijara," I said to the female with a grateful smile. "You're the best."

She grinned back, although I didn't miss the slight glimmer of sadness in her silver eyes. I bowed my head and left, my arms filled with goods. Hijara had not been the only female in the tribe to hope I would choose her as a mate, but she'd certainly been one of the most persistent. As Salha's coworker, she had often coaxed my mating-sister into speaking kindly about her to me in the hope of stirring my interest.

I returned to my dwelling, but just as I reached for the door, it swung open, startling me. Serena gasped and took a step back, looking just as surprised.

"Good morning, my mate. I didn't expect you to be up already," I said with a smile.

"I'm an early bird," she said absentmindedly, her gaze roaming over the food in the basket I carried. "Did you go get all of that for me?"

"Yes," I said, puffing out my chest. "There are fruits and nuts, but also eggs and sliced meat. We hope some of this can get close to the flavors of your homeworld."

Serena looked at the basket for another second before turning her beautiful, light brown eyes towards me. "That was so thoughtful of you," she said in a soft voice that felt like a caress. "You're very sweet, Szaro."

"My goal is to please you," I said.

"And please you most certainly do," Serena replied with a grin. She stepped aside to let me into the house. "I was on my way to take a shower, but I guess I'll have breakfast first instead."

"A shower again?" I asked, surprised. "You took one yesterday right before nightfall."

She smiled indulgently. "Most humans shower once a day, others even more often, depending on the type of work they do, where they've been, or what activity they took part in. When humans perform intense physical activity, we sweat a lot. If we don't wash after that, we end up stinking. Also, while Ordosians molt only once or twice a year, humans continually shed dead skin cells. So, if I sweat or my skin gets damp, the dead cells stick to it along with any dirt in the air. A couple of days without a shower, and I promise you will not enjoy flicking that nosy tongue of yours in my general direction."

I chuckled and instinctively flicked my tongue at her. "Well, right this instant, your scent is still quite delicious," I said sincerely.

"You flatterer," she mumbled, then turned to rummage through the basket I'd placed on the table—I suspected to hide her embarrassment. "Hmmm, this 'bacon' should produce enough fat to let me fry the eggs. Let's see how all of this tastes!"

Her enthusiasm was contagious. Serena had me bring the basket outside to the temporary counters Irco had installed next to the cooking unit. In the meantime, she fetched a plate and a couple of utensils, along with two little bottles—one with a dark grey powder and the other with tiny white grains. She turned on the cooking unit and, in no time, a rather pleasant aroma rose from the skillet in which the fatty, thin slices of meat were cooking. I wondered how much nutrition remained when she finally removed them to place them on her plate. The meat had noticeably shrunk, most of the fat having melted off it. Serena broke the eggs in the resulting oil in the skillet—making sure to keep them separated so that we would know which one came from which egg. She then sprinkled some of the grey and white powdery grains on them.

While the eggs cooked, my mate sliced some fruits, which she added to her plate. When she removed the eggs from the pan using a spatula, I was still trying to figure out how she knew they were ready *now* rather than thirty seconds ago when the color looked the same. She brought her plate of food inside the house and settled at the table while I placed the remaining fruits in the cooling unit of the kitchen.

"Do you mind if I watch?" I asked as she picked up her fork and knife. "I read that it is considered creepy."

Serena chuckled. "It *is* super creepy. But you let me watch last night. I guess it's okay for you to watch me today," she added in a teasing tone.

I snorted. "Those two hardly compare, but I will let you get away with it… this time."

Serena beamed at me and started cutting one of the slices of 'bacon' using her fork and knife. She brought the small piece to her mouth with the fork and began chewing, frowning almost immediately.

"It's bad?" I asked in a worried voice.

She shook her head. "No, not bad. Just not the taste of bacon. This is actually a bit gamey. Not unpleasant. Just unexpected," she said before cutting a piece from the second meat Hijara had provided. "Oh yeah!" Serena exclaimed with a grin as soon as she began chewing. "That's not bacon, but it's definitely closer. It's almost like ham. For lack of something else, I'd be very happy with this for breakfast in the morning."

I couldn't wipe the silly grin from my face as she moved on to the eggs. Two of them turned out to be hard to distinguish from chicken eggs but, according to my mate, the third one felt a bit more rubbery, like a duck egg. I had no idea what a duck or a chicken was, but as long as Serena had satisfactory ham and eggs for breakfast, I was content.

She finished her meal and brought her plate to the sink.

"No," I ordered when she turned on the water to start washing it. "That is my duty. In the Ordosian culture, it is the male's role to maintain the dwelling in good order, which includes building, repairing, and cleaning."

"Wow! If you're trying to make me like you, you're doing an excellent job of it right now," Serena said, looking at me with wide eyes. "But you know, in human culture, we share the chores. I don't mind—"

One stern look from me sufficed. She raised her palms in surrender, an amused expression on her face.

"Hey, if you want to hog all that *fun*, have at it! Who am I to deny you the right to indulge in your preferred forms of entertainment?"

I glared at her, which only made her laugh further. I loved the musical quality of it and the way it lit up her face. Despite her exotic features—and maybe even because of them—my mate was a beautiful female.

"I will go shower now," she said. "Be back soon!"

I set to work as soon as she left, a silly grin plastered on my face. Cleaning never bothered me. In fact, I rather enjoyed the peace and quiet, and time for reflection and introspection it provided. Furthermore, I took great pride in the cleanliness of my dwelling and having everything in proper order. After tidying Serena's cooking area and washing the dishes, I went to our rest room. It annoyed me to find she'd already fixed her bed.

A chime from my com device startled me. A quick glance caused all the warmth from the banter with my mate to fade away. I sent out a group message to all the Hunters and began putting on my battle gear. I heard Serena enter just as I was placing a dagger in my weapons belt.

The soft shuffling sound of her feet came to a stop in front of my armory's open door. The happy, carefree expression on her face vanished as soon as she saw my attire and the bag of medicines and treatments in my hand.

"That's a lot of weapons," Serena said with a sliver of tension in her voice. "Did something bad happen?"

"There is a large pack of Flayers rampaging in the northwest, near the Acales' nesting caves. As with many other species on Trangor, this month and the next is their birthing season. The Acales are at their most vulnerable during that time, not only with all the helpless young, but also because the females have all left to hunt for food, while the males look after the hatchlings. In their species, the males are smaller and weaker. They won't be able to protect their nests."

"Ouch, that bites," Serena said with a frown. "Do you think they were lured there?"

I hesitated for a second before shaking my head. "From the report I've received, there are no clear signs of treachery. The nearest Ordosian village is too far west from the Acales' lair for it to make any sense to lure in that area. There have been many reports of Flayers straying towards areas they don't normally go to. I believe they are avoiding the presence of so many hunters from your Federation, and that is pushing them further north-west. Those beasts like easy prey."

"Right..." Serena said, looking at me with a strange expression.

"What is it, my mate?" I asked.

She licked her lips, squared her shoulders, and stared me straight in the eye. "I want to go hunt them with you and the others."

I froze, taken aback by that request. A female had never joined a hunting party, but then we'd never had a human female in our midst. This request shouldn't have surprised me. In truth, I should have not only anticipated it, but offered it to her first. Tension built in my female, her shoulders becoming stiffer and a muscle jumping on her temple. I realized then that my answer could have a significant impact on our future relationship.

"Our females very rarely leave the region they were born in and never join a hunt," I said carefully. "However, unlike them, you are an experienced hunter. I do not object to you joining the hunt, BUT..." I added quickly when her face lit up, "there are certain conditions that you must commit to respect."

"I'm listening," Serena said, staring at me intently.

"You have seen how we battle the Flayers to perform as clean and merciful a kill as possible," I said. She nodded. "As you do not have a tail to help immobilize the beasts, you will need to prove you can compensate by another means without maiming the creature or causing undue harm, the alternative is to be on the stabbing duty."

"If I work with your team, I can use bolas on the non-lethal setting. They will simply immobilize the Flayer," Serena answered quickly. "I hated maiming those Flayers by the river, but I wouldn't have survived battling two mature males on my own without crippling them. My previous kills weren't as perfect as yours, but they were clean."

"I have seen your previous kills, which is the only reason I am willing to let you join us," I said, matter-of-factly. "But understand that, when on the battlefield, I am your Hunt Leader, not your mate. Following orders without question can mean life or death for the entire hunting party."

"I have no problem with following your lead," Serena said with a firm nod.

"We're in agreement then," I said.

"Yessss!!" Serena shouted, pumping both of her fists. "You're the best! Going to gear up now!"

I couldn't help chuckling and shaking my head as she dashed into our rest room to change.

"Join me outside when you're done," I said through the closed door of our room.

"Okay!" she replied, her muffled voice buzzing with excitement.

Smiling, I exited our dwelling. I should be terrified at the thought of taking my mate into danger, but only a thrill filled me. I loved that I would be sharing the main aspect of my life with my female.

However, a sense of unease settled in the pit of my stomach as I watched Raskier and my brother Mandha standing by their Drayshan. A short distance ahead, the Elders waited, ready to give us their blessing before our departure. When I allowed her to join the hunt, I had not thought of the issues my mate would face in the early days of our bonding. I needed to handle the situation carefully to avoid Serena becoming a prisoner in her new home.

Heaving a sigh, I headed towards the Elders.

"Greetings, Elders," I said to all three, although I stopped in front of Elder Krathi, our village leader.

"Greetings, Szaro," Elder Krathi responded with an almost

maternal tone. "It is unfortunate that you should be called away on a long-range hunt on the morning of your bonding."

"It is," I said with a nod. "I had hoped to show my mate the beauties of Krada, but that will have to wait."

The three Elders nodded with a commiserating smile.

"But I wish to inform you that, as an experienced hunter, my mate has requested to join us in combat, and I have agreed," I said in a firm tone.

As the Great Hunter of the tribe, I made all the decisions when it came to hunting, defending the village, or going on the offensive. The Elders only had the right to veto my decision if it represented a clear and present threat to the tribe. As expected, their faces closed off. Despite the effectiveness with which they hid their emotions, I could all but read the thoughts crossing their minds.

"I can guess what valid worries this news awakens in you," I said in an appeasing tone. "While my bonding is fresh and was initiated under less-than-perfect circumstances, there is genuine friendship and affection between my mate and me. She is an honorable female and will not seize this opportunity to attempt to flee."

I had no proof of this and yet, at a visceral level, I knew it to be true. After conversing with my mate and assessing her with his empathic abilities, Kayog had concluded that we were a perfect match. He had also vouched for her having high moral standards.

"Still, to alleviate any understandable concerns you, and anyone else in the tribe may have regarding this matter, Serena will travel with me on my Drayshan and not on her speeder," I continued. "Dagas will not allow another to ride off without me there, and Serena will never be able to make it back to the Federation base camp on foot."

Elder Krathi's face softened. "A sensible precaution," she replied. "I approve this course of action."

Relief flooded through me. I had feared a confrontation had she challenged my decision.

"I felt a strong link forming between you and the human female during last night's ceremony," the Elder continued in a pensive tone. "Are we to understand that you are pleased with your pairing?"

"The Goddess sent Serena to me," I said with conviction. "I am very pleased with the pairing."

"It warms my heart, Great Hunter," Elder Krathi replied, that same maternal expression descending on her features again.

"And mine," Elder Jyotha replied, while Elder Iskal nodded in agreement.

"Thank you, Elders," I said, grateful for their support. "We are hoping to return tonight, but I will keep you apprised of how the situation evolves."

"Do what you feel is right, Great Hunter," Elder Krathi said. "Safe journey, and may the Goddess guide your arm."

I bowed my head respectfully, then headed towards my brother who had brought out Dagas, my Drayshan. Serena came out of our dwelling before I reached him, and immediately headed towards us. I couldn't help feeling a little disappointed at the sight of the full leather hunting uniform that covered every centimeter of her beautiful skin, aside from her face and hands.

"Is everyone ready?" I asked my brother.

"Yes," he replied, although his surprised gaze remained locked on my mate approaching us. "She's coming?"

"Yes," I replied, annoyed by my defensive tone. Mandha smirked but said nothing, which only irritated me further. "Get everyone to mount up," I ordered in a snarky fashion.

Mandha's grin expanded, and I bared my fangs at him. The obnoxious wretch burst out laughing before complying with my orders. Serena stopped next to me with a questioning look.

"Give me your bag," I said, extending a hand towards her. "I will put it with mine and the others on the carrier Drayshan."

"Oh, there's no need. I can fit it in my speeder's storage since I won't have the mattress and other things in it," she countered.

"You will not be riding your speeder," I said in an apologetic tone.

"What? Why?" Serena asked, recoiling.

I gently explained the situation.

"I wouldn't run away!" Serena said, her back stiff.

"I believe you, my mate," I said softly. "I *really* do," I repeated, holding her gaze unwaveringly. That appeared to mollify her somewhat. "But do you understand why those who have had little interaction with you could have some concerns?"

Serena pinched her lips and gave me a stiff nod.

"Come on, my mate. Cheer up," I said in a teasing tone. "Who needs a speeder, anyway? You are about to become the first female of any Ordosian clan to go on a hunt *and* the first human—or off-worlder of any species for that matter—to ride a Drayshan."

"When you put it that way, it does sound like some pretty cool bragging rights," she said with the most adorable pouty lips that made me ache with the need to kiss her.

She reluctantly gave me her bag, and I went to place it with mine and the others on the carrier Drayshan. When I returned to my mate's side, she was eyeing Dagas with a mix of curiosity and suspicion.

"We're both going to ride it?" she asked in a dubious tone.

"Yes. You go on first, and I'll lie on top of you."

I burst out laughing at the flabbergasted look she gave me. It was all the funnier that I wasn't joking.

"Normally, you would simply sit or lie down in the recess on his back," I explained, pointing at it. "It allows them to carry their young until they are strong enough to walk on their own. Because of our anatomy, two adult Ordosians don't usually ride together as it's quite uncomfortable. But in your case, it will be perfect. You can lie down here and place your legs on his sides, right where it slants here. This should be comfortable for you and provide a nice support for your legs to rest on."

"And you're going to settle between my legs?" Although she worded it as a question, she was making a statement in an 'are you serious?' tone that made me want to smile again.

"My lower body will, and my tail will wrap around his hind horn," I said in a teasing voice.

"And if I'm not happy about that?" she asked.

"That is your prerogative, but you still have to comply… or remain in the village," I deadpanned.

She scrunched her face at me, making me chuckle again. Turning towards Dagas, my mate reached for one of the three recurved bones protruding from his side. With a surprising dexterity, Serena placed her right foot on the protective exoskeletal shield above his bent knee as a step to help hoist herself onto his back. Dagas turned his head to look at her with his orange eye. I caressed his hind, drawing his attention to me, making it clear it was okay to carry her. He made a chuffing sound of acceptance and turned back to face forward.

Oblivious to any of this, my mate was adjusting her position on the Drayshan, leaning down to hold on to the closest horns along the sides of his neck. Serena looked so graceful on my mount that I could have just stood there for hours admiring the tableau. To my shame though, the delicate rounded curve of her behind kept drawing my eyes. Something about it was undeniably enticing. Ordosians didn't have behinds like that, or any at all for that matter.

But beyond appreciation of that harmonious shape, less innocent thoughts filled my mind. From my research on humans, I'd discovered they could couple in a similar position, with the male standing behind his bent-over female. Ordosians couldn't do that. Our couplings had to be face to face, always the same position because of the placement of our female's slit. The thought of how creative things could get between Serena and me reawakened my nether region in a way that I really didn't need right now.

Placing one hand on the recurved bone on Dagas' side and another on his rump, I lifted myself onto his back, being careful not to squish my mate as I settled behind her. The softness of the tight curls of her black hair, neatly bound into what she called French braids, brushed against the scales of my right cheek as I leaned over her.

"Let me know if I'm crushing you," I said softly in her ear as I reached for the horns on the side of our mount's neck. "It is best if you let me handle the horns. You can hold onto my arms if you wish. But it will likely be more comfortable for you to simply rest your palms on his shoulders."

"Okay," Serena said, shifting under me.

Her behind rubbed against my pelvic area in the most exquisite torture. Although I hated how much her hunting outfit covered her skin, it was turning out to be a relief that I couldn't feel her naked heat under my chest.

"I'm good. This should be fine and is surprisingly comfortable," my mate added, sounding rather stunned.

"I'm glad to hear it," I said, genuinely pleased. "Do not hesitate to tell me if you feel discomfort at any point."

"Will do," she said with a nod.

I gave the signal to the others who were patiently waiting, and we finally departed.

CHAPTER 10
SERENA

I'd never been one to suffer from motion sickness. The steady rocking back and forth of Dagas as it raced through the woods at dizzying speed wasn't responsible for my insides having liquified and turned into a bubbling pool of lava. Szaro's firm body rubbing against mine with each galloping step of the Drayshan was driving me insane. His wretched tongue flicking from time to time, the smug smile stretching his lips, and the occasional teasing glance he would steal my way only confirmed he knew how this ride affected me.

I tried to ignore the intoxicating feel of him wrapped around me and focused on the breathtaking view of our surroundings. Thanks to the inclined position in which we lay on the Drayshan's back, I didn't have to strain my neck to keep my head up and look ahead.

We left the Krada region, clearing the valley where I'd been hunting alongside their border and moved further northwest into new-to-me territories. Szaro began pointing out various landmarks and gave me some background information and stories about the local flora and fauna. I was so caught up in this improvised guided tour, further lulled by the hypnotic sound of his deep voice with that purring rattling sound, that the distant screech of a Flayer startled me.

Szaro tensed behind me. The team slowed their mounts, angling them towards the mountain range we'd been following. Some of the Ordosians dismounted their Drayshans before they even came to a full stop. None of them bothered with the carrier Drayshan and rushed towards the shouting beasts a short distance ahead as soon as Szaro nodded at them. The speed with which they slithered away made me wonder why they bothered with mounts.

I ran to the carrier to pick up my bag. Szaro removed his staff but didn't affix it to a harness across his back, and joined me. I expected him to race to catch up with the others, instructing me to follow at my own pace. Instead, he turned his back to me.

"Hop on my back," he ordered.

I froze for half a second, then slipped on my backpack and came to stand behind Szaro, my legs on each side of his tail. He closed his hood, folding each flap against his head as I wrapped my arms around his neck.

"Can you hold my staff?" he asked, extending it to me.

I grabbed it with my right hand, and Szaro slipped both of his behind my knees to lift my legs to his sides, carrying me piggyback.

"Hang on tightly," he ordered.

Before I could answer, Szaro surged forward, carrying me effortlessly and moving at the same astonishing speed as the others, as if I weighed nothing. For a brief instant, I wondered at the Drayshans that had been left behind without being tied to anything. Did the Ordosians not fear they would wander off or run away from fright? But a look over my shoulder showed the beasts all standing idly, apparently unfazed by the distant roaring of the Flayers.

Heart pounding, I tried to make out what was happening ahead as Szaro swayed from side to side, gliding in between the sparse trees at the edge of the forest like an ice skater would. We stopped about fifty meters from where Mandha and four Ordosians were fighting the first Flayer.

"Arm yourself and come assist my unit when you are ready," Szaro ordered before dashing towards a group to the left of Mandha.

A dozen or so Flayers were moving north towards the clearing, which led to a massive cave in the mountain. Actually, it didn't fit the description of a cave since it was open on both ends, creating, rather, a tunnel that opened onto the cliff above the river below. At least twenty meters deep, the side walls of the open cave overflowed with fresh hatchlings chirping in the countless nests built directly into the recesses of the stone.

I quickly removed my weapons from my backpack, including six bolas, and hooked them onto my belt. I tossed my backpack to the side and ran towards Szaro's position, a bola in hand, ready to be thrown. Sadly, by the time I got close enough, he was already severing its spine. The four males swiftly moved to another target. This time, I managed to throw my bola, shackling the Flayer's two front legs, seconds before the Ordosians reached it. Without blinking, the three males each immobilize two of the beast's six remaining legs with their tails, then Szaro went in for the kill. I proudly lifted my chin at the approving grin he cast my way.

Just as I was spinning my second bola, thinking how obscenely easy this was proving to be, three Flayers charged forward as one. My team scattered out of their path, but the beast on the left chased after one of them. I let my bola fly. It caught the creature's hind legs in extremis, but it was enough to trip it. It fell flat on its face, giving our teammate a chance to escape… or so I thought.

I realized too late that he'd in fact pretended to be slower to lure the beast away from the nests. Impeded though it was by my bola restraining two of its legs, the Flayer got back up and resumed chasing its target with a clunky, yet swift gait. Up ahead, Szaro and the other two members of my team were also attempting to draw the Flayers away from the cave. But the Acales males protecting the nests—in a pointless attempt to scare them away—rushed towards the beasts. This only made the Flayers hungrier for easy prey.

Realizing they wouldn't be able to get the creatures to stray from their current targets, Szaro and the others converged on the biggest of the two. I grabbed another bola, but just as I was about to throw it, the sight of the birds ineffectively attacking the 'smaller' beast suddenly triggered an old memory. On instinct, I launched my bola at that creature instead of the one my team was rushing.

I yanked out the whistle from the attachment pocket on my left arm, swiftly entered the program setting on the interface, and blew in it. The Acales jerked their heads towards me, a few of them appearing to want to come to me before resuming their attacks on the Flayer that was getting back on its feet. It swiped its scythed limbs at them, cutting down too many Acales. I blew in my flute again, my fingers moving over the holes, modulating the sound.

And then it worked.

The Acales collectively emitted a loud screech then flew towards me, the Flayer hot on their trail. I locked the pattern into the flute and continued blowing the rally call as I ran towards Mandha's team which had defeated the other nearby Flayers and was running our way. Heart pounding into my throat at the sound of the beast quickly approaching behind me, I turned around only long enough to fling another bola. It completely missed its mark. However, in its attempt to avoid it, the Flayer dodged to the side, the legs I'd previously restrained making it lose its footing. It fell onto its stomach, its momentum causing it to slide a short distance.

It never had a chance to get back up as Mandha's team descended upon it.

Ignoring my wobbly knees, I continued blowing into the flute and lured the Acales back into the cave while Raskier's team and Szaro's handled the last two Flayers. Once inside the cave, I stopped the rally call. The Acales flew in circles over and around me for a few seconds then, one by one, they returned to their nests.

I walked out of the cave, worry quickly replacing the adrenaline coursing through my veins as I watched Szaro approach me with a severe expression. I swallowed hard and braced.

"You didn't follow my orders," he said sternly.

"I know. I'm sorry. I didn't mean to go off on my own," I said in an apologetic tone. "It's just that when I saw the Acales, I realized they looked almost identical to the Shivarees, a species I've done protection jobs for in the past. And I got this hunch that the whistle could spare them from getting slaughtered. I acted on instinct."

"Your instinct was correct, and you did save most of the males," he conceded, his voice still as serious. "But if you had been wrong, and worst still, if Mandha's team had not been done with the beast they'd been fighting when you began luring, many of you could have been injured or killed."

"I know," I said, hanging my head in shame. "I truly am sorry."

"I know you are," he said, his tone softening. "I do not fault you for adapting to the changing situation of a battle, and I do not expect blind obedience. You actually made the right call, just not the right way."

I recoiled, getting whiplash from the sudden turn around. "Not the right way?"

"You correctly assessed that the rest of our team and I could handle our beast without your assistance, but you didn't plan where you would go with the second one, or who would assist you once you got the Acales away from it. I believe you acted the same way when you rescued Salha and Eicu. You saw vulnerable beings in danger, and you rushed headfirst to the rescue without much concern for your own safety. You have a big heart, my mate. But you cannot help anyone if you get yourself killed in the process."

My cheeks burned, and I scrunched my face. "Right. I may have a tendency to act first and think later under certain circumstances," I said in a small voice. "I'll work on that."

"See that you do, my mate. I will not be widowed," he replied teasingly. "You did well," he added with an approving glimmer in his eyes.

"More than well," Mandha exclaimed from behind him, as he approached us with the others. "That was impressive. What was that sound?"

"It's the Shivarees' rally call," I said, standing straighter at the praise, echoed by the others as they joined us. "They are a bird species from Marvix 5, a small planet in the Crastar sector. They are quite similar in appearance to these Acales. On our way here, Szaro told me the Acale males are smaller and protect the nests while the females are the hunters and fighters of their species."

"Like those Shivarees?" Raskier asked.

"Exactly like those Shivarees," I replied with a nod. "When their nest is under attack, the group of defending females will emit that cry so that the males and their young can rally to that position to be protected while the other females go to battle. The pitch isn't quite the same, which is why I had to modify it a bit, but I got it close enough to work."

"How did you guess that was the problem?" Szaro asked with obvious curiosity. "How did you know what pitch to set?"

"That was also a hunch, to be honest. Their shriek is a few tones deeper than that of the Shivarees. So I lowered the call accordingly."

“Smart female,” Raskier said, his eyes gleaming with the same admiration I could see in the other hunters’ eyes. “Your timely intervention saved this species from returning to the brink of extinction.”

“This is their only nest?” I exclaimed.

“No,” Szaro replied, “but it is the biggest. You are proving to be a natural Guardian, like the rest of us.”

“Thank you,” I said, basking in their collective approval. I’d been so scared of royally fucking up.

“But now we must tend to the wounded and see if there is any additional threat lurking nearby,” Szaro said, sobering.

He looked at Mandha simply nodded in the way people with years of working together no longer needed to speak to understand what the other wanted or needed. Mandha gestured with his head for two of his teammates to follow, and they hastened to where we left the Drayshans. Szaro then spoke a few words in Ordosian to Raskier who nodded as well. His team and one other immediately headed south through the woods. To my shock, Raskier lagged behind, going from one fallen Flayer to the next to mark them with a beacon gun.

“We’ve got to claim your kills,” Szaro said with a grin.

I burst out laughing. “You guys are amazing.”

“No, my mate, *you* are amazing,” he said before raising a hand to caress my cheek.

He seemed as surprised as I was by the tender gesture. Although I didn’t pull away, he dropped his hand almost immediately thereafter. His suddenly embarrassed look made me conscious that our team and the two remaining members of Mandha’s team were still present, observing us. The approving look in their eyes communicated their pleasure that our union appeared to be on the right track. It hadn’t been a calculated move, but it didn’t hurt our pretense that we were giving it an honest go.

Is it a pretense though?

Not from Szaro's point of view. My husband was definitely playing for keeps. It disturbed me how quickly he was making me want to reconsider my own stance on this.

"Recover your bolas," Szaro said. "Everyone else, let's get to work."

I nodded and went to recover my weapons. Before joining the males, I ran the short distance to where I had tossed my backpack and shoved my weapons back inside. As I approached the cave, I was shocked to hear the rattling of the Ordosians' tails. A number of Acale males had taken flight, circling in a menacing fashion as Szaro and the others approached the nests. Gradually, the birds landed, losing all aggressive stance despite the Ordosians closing in on them. When I entered the cave a powerful sense of peace washed over me.

The rattling is doing this!

But how? During the wedding, the entire crowd had shaken their rattles, and it hadn't affected me. Then again, when Szaro had rattled his right next to my ear, I'd instantly gone into heat.

The pattern had been different.

No… not just the pattern but the pitch as well. I watched in fascination as the Ordosians examined the birds one by one, placing the wounded ones aside to be treated. The creatures docilely submitted to them.

Mandha and his teammates returned with the Drayshans. They brought the bags of medicine from the carrier so the males could treat the wounded. To my surprise, Mandha carried a huge silver bag with the logo of the Federation and started filling it with the remains of the dead Acales. Once done, he sealed it, which automatically sucked the air out of the bag, thereby preserving the bodies in their current state. He placed it next to one of the dead Flayers, inside the protective dome created by my beacon.

I joined Szaro and, for the next few hours, I assisted him and the others in caring for the wounded birds. An hour into it, my heart leapt in my chest at the sight of the Federation shuttle landing in the clearing to recover the remains of the Flayers. The extraction team worked swiftly and efficiently under the watchful eyes of the Ordosians.

As they were coming back out of the shuttle to pick up one of the last two beasts, one of the agents noticed my presence. Shock gave way to pity in his eyes. I could only imagine what kind of wild speculations were going on at the base camp as to my fate. I beamed at him and waved in a friendly manner to express that all was well. That seemed to throw him for a loop, which only made my smile broaden. I would kill to know what tale he would tell the others once he returned.

Thirty minutes before we were finished, Raskier returned with those who had accompanied him into the forest. By then, the sun was setting on the horizon, and my stomach was clamoring for food. I munched on an energy bar under the amused gazes of the Ordosians.

"No wonder humans eat so often," Mandha said teasingly as I drank a sip of water. "There is no way that tiny bar provided sufficient sustenance. These birds eat bigger meals."

"That bar may look small, but it's surprisingly filling," I deadpanned. "It's not the best meal, but it's practical, and I'm actually quite full now."

"And you'll be hungry again in a few hours," Raskier retorted. "Can't you store reserves so that you do not need to eat for a few days?"

"Our stomach doesn't have much room, and we have a high metabolism," I replied. "Anything in my stomach will be processed in a matter of hours, some things take even less time depending on what they are."

"Our stomach is also relatively small," Mandha said while giving me an assessing look. "But even though they are slender, your legs are long. Can you not store food there to be digested at a later time?"

I burst out laughing, immediately slapping a hand over my mouth and feeling horrible at the thought I might have offended him.

"I'm sorry. I'm not laughing at you, but the thought of having food storage in our legs is very funny," I said with a sheepish expression. "I'm assuming that means you guys… errr Ordosians store food in your tail?"

They all nodded.

"Wow, okay. That explains a few things," I said, feeling a little silly. "But no. We don't have any food storage anywhere. Our legs are only bones surrounded by skin, tendons, muscles and nerves."

Having twenty pairs of reptilian male eyes all staring at my legs had me squirming in no time.

"So… what now?" I asked to shift the attention away from my legs and eating habits.

"There are more packs moving northwest," Szaro said. "I've received a couple of reports from my father. Their scouts had to deal with a number of Flayers but are keeping an eye on the packs beyond their normal range. They will keep us informed. Considering that it's already late, and as we'll likely have to come back to this sector tomorrow, traveling two hours to get back to the village doesn't make sense. I suggest we stay the night."

"In the usual cave?" Mandha asked.

Szaro nodded.

I stared at Szaro in shock. First, I didn't realize his father was still around. As he hadn't introduced me to either of his parents in the village after our wedding, I'd assumed they had both passed away, not that they lived with a different tribe. And two hours?! Had I been in such a lustful daze on our way here not to realize we'd been traveling that long?

While excited at the thought of sleeping in the wild with the Ordosians, I regretted not bringing my inflatable mattress.

Sleeping on the hard surface of the cave would leave me sore and aching in the morning.

We traveled a short distance west of the Acales nests to a rather impressive cave. The large entrance split into two winding corridors with little nooks along the way. Szaro led me down the left branch. For a moment, I almost pulled out my flashlight as the darkness thickened around us, but light quickly reappeared a short distance ahead. We reached a dead-end with a natural skylight in the ceiling of the cave. The ground of the relatively large, roughly oval space, maybe four meters wide and six meters long, was mostly even and made of packed dirt.

To my surprise, the others didn't follow us to the back, most of them settling in the entrance or in some of the nooks at the beginning of the corridor.

"We are newly bonded," Szaro said in a gentle voice, guessing the thoughts crossing my mind. "They are granting us some privacy."

"I see," I said, heat creeping back up on my cheeks.

I cast a look around the barren space, wondering where I would settle down.

"I would like you to lie on me," Szaro said matter-of-factly. "The ground is too hard for you. I should have anticipated that we might stay overnight and told you to bring your mattress."

I tried to reassure him. "It's okay, I can survive one night on the hard floor."

"It might be more than one night," Szaro countered. "Do not worry. I am not trying to take advantage. And you should find my tail quite comfortable to sleep on."

"I know you're not," I mumbled. "But how would that even work?"

He folded his tail into a spiral, turning it effectively into a rather large 'cushion' that I could curl up on.

"But you use your tail as your own cushion," I argued weakly, remembering how he slept last night.

"Ordosians deliberately sleep on a flat and hard surface," Szaro said in a 'don't be silly' tone. "I do not need the cushion. You do. Now, stop arguing, female. Hunt Leader's orders."

"Ah!" I said with playful defiance, similar to his falsely commanding tone. "We're not hunting right now. You can't dictate what I do."

"Fine," he grumbled. "Then comply to save your mate from an entire night of being tormented by guilt for making you sleep in inadequate conditions due to his lack of foresight."

"Wow, you really play dirty!" I said, shaking my head at him with a chuckle.

"I do what I must to protect you from yourself," he deadpanned.

"I don't need protecting," I countered.

"You need to let me take care of you. Come to me, my mate." He extended a hand towards me.

"Hang on," I replied.

I kicked off my boots, then removed the vest and pants of my hunting uniform, and carefully folded them on top of my backpack. When I turned back towards Szaro, the way he looked at me made my knees wobble. I took a glance at myself, wondering what had triggered such a reaction. While they did hug my curves, my sports bra and training pants weren't suggestive in their design. When I looked back at Szaro, the neutral expression on his face gave me whiplash. Had I imagined his previous reaction?

Once again, he extended his hand towards me. This time, I went to him. He leaned his upper body to the side, resting his head on his hand. It felt strange to climb on top of him like and even more so as I curled on my side, facing him. The softness of his scales against my skin left me reeling. But his happy smile erased any last hesitation I still held. I folded my left arm under my head.

"Okay, you win. You're a very comfortable mattress," I said in a whisper.

I didn't know why I'd lowered my voice like that, but lying on top of him, our faces so close to each other seemed to call for it.

He didn't respond with the teasing reply I expected. His face just softened with a tender expression, and he gently caressed my cheek.

CHAPTER 11
SERENA

That gentle, innocent touch sufficed to reignite a fire in the pit of my stomach. I loved the feel of him around me, the tenderness mixed with wonder in his eyes whenever he looked at me, and the careful, respectful way in which he always touched me. Surprisingly, I also liked his smell—earthy and woodsy, evoking a wild, carefree run through the forest, danger, and power, but also home and stability.

"Tell me about yourself, Serena Bello," Szaro said as he moved his hand away from my face.

"There isn't much to say about me, really," I said, pursing my lips as I pondered what info felt relevant. "I am the oldest of two. My sister is my opposite in all the ways that matter, but she's the perfect child for my parents."

"You do not get along with your family?" Szaro asked with a slight frown.

"I wouldn't quite say that. I love my family, and I try to visit them every month or two. When I can't, we communicate through vidcom. But we don't have a lot in common. They're very corporate, high-tech, and high society. I'm like a wild animal. I need to be surrounded by nature, by things that are simple and authentic. With socialites, everything is about appearance. You feel obligated to act a certain way or do certain things because that's what is expected. Not the case with animals. You know exactly where you stand."

"Yes, animals can usually smell or sense deception," Szaro said. "Am I to understand your parents disapprove of you being a hunter?"

I snorted. "That's the understatement of the century. They thought I was going to do it for a while and grow out of it, like I have with other things I've pursued," I said, shaking my head. "When they realized I really loved hunting, they tried to use their influence to get me a high-ranking position on the board of the Federation. And it would have worked, too, but I refused."

"Why?" Szaro asked, genuinely surprised. "Isn't it a position of honor?"

"It is, but that would mean staying at their headquarters behind a desk, meeting with 'important' people and doing all that socialite stuff I specifically don't want to do," I said with disgust. "In my parents' mind, I should be chasing a big salary with little danger. Instead, I'm going into the field, putting my safety at risk, often for uncertain compensation. But I love this life."

"You love killing dangerous beasts?" he asked.

I recoiled, offended by the question. There had been no accusation in his tone, but the intensity in his eyes hinted that he would weigh my answer.

"No," I said forcefully. "I don't *love* killing anything. Is there a predator part of me that enjoys the thrill of danger and defeating my opponent? Yes. But I don't hunt for sport or for fun. I started out as an exobiologist assistant in a regional park of Oraya. A flood then a mudslide sent the predatory packs from the north down into the park. Countless vulnerable species got decimated. I was helpless to protect them. That's when I learned how to hunt."

"So, you kill to protect," Szaro said in a soft voice.

"Yes," I said, proudly lifting my chin. "But, contrary to their name, the Federation Hunts aren't always about killing. Often, it's about capturing creatures and relocating them, be they pacific ones in jeopardy or rampaging predators so they won't threaten vulnerable species. On Oraya, had a hunting team made it there in time, that's what they would have done."

"It is honorable, my mate," he said with warmth in his eyes. "But do you truly want to travel forever?"

"No, not forever," I conceded. "The past few years have allowed me to discover worlds and species that I never could have imagined. It has been beyond wonderful. Eventually, I would like to settle somewhere and retire as an exotic beast breeder, a trainer, or a wildlife ranger in a massive park."

"Then search no more, Serena. This is exactly what we are, and you will never find a greater park than this one," he said in a deep voice. "The entire planet is our playground. You haven't seen exotic until you've explored all of Trangor. I promise, you will fall in love with this place… and with me."

I gasped at his boast. But if today was any indication, he might just be right about me falling in love with this planet.

And with him…

"Enough about me. I want to hear about you," I said to hide my embarrassment. "You mentioned your father earlier. I didn't realize he was still alive."

Szaro grinned. "My father will outlive all of us. He is the Great Hunter of the Tulma village and probably the greatest of our time," he said proudly. "I was born there. I was first, Mandha second. I have three other siblings that live with my parents there, another brother and two sisters."

"Oh wow! Why did you leave?" I asked.

"Because the village didn't need another Great Hunter," he said matter-of-factly. "But also because I didn't find a mate in my village. It is common for males who do not feel the call of their mate to move from one village to the next, until they either find a life companion or the one they will bond with."

An uneasy feeling settled in the pit of my stomach. "But you settled in Krada… Had you found a companion? Did I get in the way of—"

"No! No, my mate," Szaro said with an amused expression. "I had only planned on staying for a month, but some pretty scary beasts developed a serious case of rage. I joined the hunters in battle. At the end, they asked me to become their Great Hunter."

"Nice! You must have really impressed them! But… what of the previous Great Hunter?" I asked. "That must have been awkward."

"The previous Great Hunter suggested it," Szaro said smugly. "It was Raskier, Elder Krathi's grandson."

"No!" I exclaimed in disbelief.

He chuckled. "Yes. We are the guardians of this world, Serena. Our species doesn't have currency. Everyone simply does what their respective skills allow them to do so that we can look after all the forms of life the Goddess has entrusted to our care. Trangor needs us, and we need her." His gaze roamed over my features, and he gently caressed my cheek again. "And in my heart, I know that it needs you, too. Tomorrow, I will show you more of its beauty. But for now, we should rest as we will rise early."

"All right," I whispered.

To my shock, Szaro leaned forward, his face stopping a hair's breadth from mine. Without hesitation, I closed the distance between us and pressed my lips to his. I didn't know what I had expected, but the tender kiss we exchanged, devoid of lust and passion, felt right. Szaro broke the kiss after a few seconds, looked at me affectionately, then pressed his lips again to my forehead.

"Pleasant dreams to you, my mate."

"And to you, Szaro."

I curled up a little closer to his torso and felt his strong arm close around me as I surrendered to sleep.

~

I growled in irritation at the hand gently shaking me and snuggled further. My mattress shaking in tandem with rumbling laughter pierced the fog of sleep that clung to me. I heaved a frustrated sigh as the most wonderful sleep I'd experienced in a while slipped away from me. I inhaled deeply, the delectable earthy, woodsy scent of Szaro filling my nose.

My eyes snapped open as I finally remembered that I was sleeping on top of his wrapped tail. Furthermore, I'd somehow managed to slip my arm around his waist and bury my face in his neck. I almost pulled away in the panicked way of the guilty.

Why the heck should I?

He was my husband. *He* insisted I sleep on him, and there was nothing wrong with enjoying a good night's sleep.

"You're seriously the best mattress ever," I mumbled, rubbing my face on the soft scales of his neck before trying to snuggle some more.

Szaro emitted that happy rattling laughter again, his hand gently caressing my back. "I am pleased to hear it, my mate," he said in a joyous tone. "It truly pains me to wake you, but we must get going. I promise to play mattress for you again tonight."

"I will hold you to it," I said grumpily while forcing myself up.

I stretched and rubbed the sleep from my face.

"The others are checking up on the Acales. I will go see how things are going while you dress," Szaro said.

I nodded, and quickly put my hunting suit back on. As I had not brought a comb or brush, I unbraided my hair, wet it a little with some of the water from a bottle in my backpack to keep it moisturized, and used my fingers to detangle it as much as possible. Then, I did my usual hunt hairdo, a French braid on each side. I had just begun braiding the second side when Szaro returned. He watched me with a fascinated expression.

When I finished, he approached and carefully ran his fingers over the plaits.

"That is beautiful and so perfectly executed," he said pensively. "How do you manage without a mirror?"

"Practice, my dear," I said with a smug grin. "Did the others abandon us?"

"No, but they're about to," he replied playfully. "Come," he added, taking my hand.

A voice at the back of my head said I should probably pull my hand away, not indulge in these kinds of tender interactions that would deepen our bond. But I silenced it. Something had happened last night. Or rather, something had been happening since our Ordosian wedding ceremony. Yesterday's hunt and last night only reinforced it. I didn't know if this marriage could work, or if I even wanted it to. I just no longer wanted to fight whatever was happening between us. Let the chips fall where they may.

To my shock, we exited the cave to find the others were indeed about to abandon us. I cast an inquisitive look towards Szaro.

"They are going to scout ahead," he explained. "You and I are going to check on some vulnerable species in the area to make sure they aren't facing any challenges during their birthing season."

"Sounds like a plan!" I said, excitement bubbling inside of me.

When he saw me pulling out an energy bar for breakfast, Szaro told me to save it. He had a different meal in mind for me.

Intrigued, I complied and wished the others goodbye as they headed southwest.

We got onto Dagas, Szaro hooking my backpack onto the Drayshan's hind horn, and we rode west parallel to the mountain range. I nearly purred at the sensation of my husband lying on my back, rekindling naughty thoughts as the beast's movements rocked us back and forth.

To my shock, we entered a hidden passage I never would have noticed as the large boulders appeared to create a seamless formation. It was wide enough to allow two Drayshans to travel comfortably side by side. The short passage, maybe a hundred meters long on a curve, opened on a hidden orchard straight out of a fairy tale and leading down to the river.

Szaro stopped the Drayshan and dismounted. After helping me down, he took my hand and led me towards the orchard. The trees vaguely resembled short pines—the top no more than one meter above my head—but with clearly spaced out rows of branches. Bright blue fruits, shaped like pinecones, dangled in pairs from the branches. Each pair shared a single spiraling stem that reminded me of the albuca plant. I couldn't tell if the sounds emanating from the trees were birds chirping or cricket-like insects singing.

As we approached, Szaro began rattling his tail with that appeasing sound that instantly made me feel relaxed. I then noticed the nests atop each branch, woven from the tree's needles. Within each nest, five tiny featherless baby birds with the tail of a seahorse were chirping blindly to be fed. Each one was no bigger than my thumb, and their translucent skin showed their vulnerable organs within.

"They're so small," I said, my chest constricting for them. "Did they hatch too early?"

"No, my mate," Szaro whispered. "These are young Scogas right after their first birth. They hatch three days after their mother lays their eggs, feed for two days, then go into a cocoon for two weeks."

"A cocoon?!" I exclaimed, blown away. "But—"

A buzzing sound drew my attention, interrupting me. For a split second, I thought my eyes were playing tricks on me, then I noticed an adult Scoga shedding its camouflage. It had so perfectly blended with the background and the tree that I never would have been able to spot it. All around us, countless other adults were also coming out of hiding, no doubt thanks to Szaro's calming rattle. Brightly colored, the one in front of me had the body of a bee hummingbird, a gecko head, and a seahorse tail. Hovering in place, it rubbed its head against the surprisingly soft fruits hanging over the nest.

"Do not make any sudden movements, or it will frighten the mother again, and she may go back into hiding. Her young must eat constantly for the next two days to have a chance to survive their transformation. The parents rotate in six-hour shifts, allowing the other to rest and eat before coming back."

Even as he spoke, the blue fruits started turning a whitish color, and the spiral stem between them unfurled, straightening and widening until it dangled almost like a hose over the nest. Seconds later, a fragrant white paste—with a citrusy scent that made me immediately think of a key-lime pie—began dripping into the nest. The young greedily devoured it.

"You've got to be kidding me…" I whispered, unsure if I wanted to burst out laughing or be shocked.

Szaro gave me a confused look. I shook my head to say it wasn't important.

"You've got to taste it. It is extremely nutritious," he said enthusiastically.

I hesitated. "Oh… I don't know about that."

He ignored my protests and, still holding my hand, lured me to a different tree. No chirping emanated from it, and no adults hovered around. Instead, the tiny shapes of the hatchlings had begun covering themselves in a thick cocoon of a color matching perfectly the needles of the tree. With no conscious Scoga around to startle, Szaro reached for a pair of blue fruits and began massaging them.

"Take the funnel as it unfolds, and hold it in front of your mouth," he said. "Do not worry, it will not choke you. It comes in small spurts."

That did it.

I burst out laughing, cringing the whole time, and reached for his hands to pull them away from the fruits. His confusion only made me laugh harder.

"What's wrong? Do you not want to taste it?" he asked.

"Sweetie, I realize this means nothing to you, but this whole thing is very awkward for me," I said, feeling silly about my schoolgirl reaction. "Humans have an expression to describe the state a man can be in. We call it 'having blue balls.'"

Szaro's eyes widened, and his head jerked towards the fruits. He stared at them for a moment, a series of emotions flitting rapidly over his features. I didn't think he would make the association, considering how anatomically different Ordosians were to humans, but…

"Men only? Not women?" he asked.

"Men only," I said with a nod.

Szaro forced his gaze away from the fruits to give me the strangest look, making me want to squirm.

"Are you seriously comparing the rugal fruit to human male genitalia?" he asked, disbelievingly.

"Hey! You managed to make the association. So, clearly there is a resemblance!" My tone was slightly defensive, even as I fought the urge to chuckle.

"Only because I cannot think of any other balls a human male could possess that a female doesn't," Szaro argued. "Your anatomy books do not show them to be blue, or that your males have such a long and narrow penis."

"Granted," I said, still fighting the urge to laugh through my embarrassment. "But having blue balls means that the man is aroused but denied release. Watching you massaging them to make the stem—or funnel—'hard' so that it could release was just more than I could handle."

"You are disturbed," he said, looking at me like I'd grown a second head.

I chuckled sheepishly. "This is nothing. Humans can become extremely silly when it comes to sex jokes."

He stared at me for a moment longer, apparently at a loss. "This is not a sexual organ. It is a fruit that produces a highly nutritious paste," he said at last. "It can provide you with proper sustenance and enhance your immune system."

"Okay," I said, sobering. "I will taste some of your rugal paste. But no more ball massaging for you."

I didn't know why I was having such juvenile fun teasing him like this. I was just relieved that, although he didn't get why this was so comical to me, he was becoming amused by the situation. But as I began to massage the balls and opened my mouth under the unfolding stem, the look on his face changed. Despite reminding me the rugals were fruits, he could no longer see them simply as such. I'd ruined them for him… and I had no shame about it.

That said, whatever mischievous spirit had taken possession of me, when that white goop landed on my tongue and the most divine, creamy, sweet, and citrusy flavors exploded on my taste buds, the voluptuous moan that tore out of my throat was definitely not planned. With a will of their own, my hands went to town on those balls, squeezing out every drop. I vaguely heard Szaro burst out laughing, but I didn't care. When that first pair of rugals ran out, I moved on to the next under my wretched husband's smug grin. Halfway through the fourth, I had to call it quits. Just like my energy bars, that creamy substance was extremely filling. Still, I stopped with major reluctance.

"I told you it was good," Szaro said proudly.

"And you were right," I conceded, still licking my lips. "But how do you know? I thought Ordosians only ate meat?"

"It's true, but rugal paste is fed to someone too sick to eat normally or to handle solid food. And as mentioned before, it helps reinforce the immune system." He then pointed at the chrysalis of the little cocooning Scogas. "Once they emerge, the shells they leave behind are also good for consumption. They possess great regenerative properties. The pharmaceutical firms of the United Planets Organization are especially eager to acquire these. It allows them to produce a cream that regrows skin on the severely burned and even regenerates limbs in certain species."

"Wow! That's wonderful! But how are they going to get them when all of these hatch?" I asked. "This is part of the forbidden zone. Are the people from the extraction team allowed to come here?"

"No," he said with a finality that made it clear no off-worlder was allowed in this sanctuary. "The extraction teams get special permission to only go specifically where a Flayer has been killed so that there is no waste. They are in and out in minutes. In a couple of weeks, we will return to harvest the empty shells and add them to the other things we give them."

"I hope they pay you for that."

"No. What for?" Szaro asked in an amused tone. "I told you, my mate, we do not have currency here. We do not need it."

"But you could acquire new technology to accelerate the development of your own, eventually build your own spaceship and visit the stars," I argued.

"Ordosians do not leave Trangor," Szaro said, this time taking on a very serious expression. "We are bound to this planet, and it is bound to us. We have no wish to explore the worlds beyond. As long as the off-worlders do not threaten the balance of life here, we are happy to freely give them what would otherwise go to waste, but only if they are using it for good. The minute they break our covenant, we will not be so nice."

That hardness in his voice and the merciless glimmer in his eyes gave me a cold shiver.

"But enough about this," he said, his face softening. "We have some exploring to do. Hop on my back, Serena, and we'll be on our way."

"Should I get my backpack?"

"You won't need it. We will return soon enough, and the area is safe," he replied.

I gladly climbed on his back, and he carried me, piggyback-style, as he exited the hidden valley and reentered the forest, following a path west. For the next few hours, Szaro showed me countless wonders—plants and animals whose existence I never could have imagined. From time to time, he would stop to fix something and help some creature in distress like putting a fallen nestling back in its nest or aiding the alien version of Bambi's mom to push out a baby that needed to be turned. He even trimmed some of the giant leaves of a tree whose name I don't remember as they blocked the light needed by the berry bushes below that would feed the scurrying creatures in the underbrush.

By the time we returned to the hidden valley, the afternoon was already waning. And yet, I could have gone on forever. When they weren't performing population control as was currently the case with the Flayers, the Ordosian Hunters did what Szaro and I did today, simply scout their planet to take care of it. I could definitely see myself doing that.

"We will spend the night here in the valley, or at the cave," Szaro said when I got off his back. "Your choice."

"Shouldn't we be joining with the others?" I asked.

"Unnecessary. They have things under control. We will meet them in Tulma tomorrow, and I will introduce you to my parents and other siblings," Szaro said with a grin.

My stomach dropped. As much as I was curious about his family, I was nowhere near ready to meet the parents.

"Do not worry, my mate. All will be well," he said in a reassuring tone. "For now, what do you say we go swim in the river? It is not a shower, but I know you like to wash often."

"Are you hinting that I stink?" I asked, falsely glaring at him.

He laughed, flicked his tongue at me, and shook his head. "Your scent is still delicious to me. Come."

When he extended his hand towards me, I thought he simply wanted to hold it like he'd been doing all day, but he drew me to him and picked me up in his arms instead. I yelped and instinctively wrapped my arms around his neck. Our eyes met and he gave me that tender look again that seriously messed with my head. He was growing on me way too quickly.

I never saw him lowering his face towards mine. But when our lips met, I responded willingly. It was too brief. Eyes locked with mine, Szaro carried me like a bride to the shore, the slight swaying motion of his movements as he glided on the grass, gently rocking me.

For a moment, I thought he was going to enter the water with me still in his arms and fully dressed. But he stopped by a large rock and set me back on my feet. He carefully removed his bracers and other attachments and placed them on top of the rock. I removed my boots and leather suit and stood before him in my sports bra and training shorts. Szaro gave me the strangest look. In that instant, I'd have given every credit to my name to be able to read his mind.

"I will grant you privacy," he said in a gentle tone.

Without waiting for my response, he turned around and headed a good hundred meters to the left before entering the water. I headed straight ahead to the water, removing my top and bottom, that also served as my undies—yeah, I had a thing for going commando. I entered the crystalline water, surprised to find it a lot less cold than I had expected. It wasn't lukewarm, just cool, maybe around 12-15°C. I washed my clothes the best I could, wrung out as much water as possible, then hung them on a low branch of a nearby tree.

I wondered if Szaro was watching me from a distance as I strutted about buck naked. That thought thrilled me. I didn't question my current emotions. Walking back to the water, I cast a glance in his direction. Szaro was swimming around, making impressive jumps out of the water like a dolphin. My gaze never strayed from his acrobatic dance as I took my sweet time washing myself.

I couldn't recall starting to swim in his direction. When he suddenly stopped, turned, and looked at me, I realized there were only a dozen meters between us. He'd folded his hood while playing in the water, probably to make himself more aerodynamic. But he deployed it again, expanding it to the maximum as he swam towards me—or rather glided on the water. He wasn't using his arms, which he kept loosely alongside his body, propelling himself with his tail.

To my surprise, instead of coming directly to me, he started circling me, like a shark around its prey, the radius narrowing with each revolution. He finally came to a stop, inches from me, but without touching me.

"You are naked, Serena," he said, his voice deeper than I could recall, and the slight rattling sound that accompanied it even more pronounced than usual.

"I am," I acknowledged.

"You are forfeiting your privacy?" he insisted.

"I am," I repeated.

Lifting one hand, treading water with the other, I caressed the left inner side of his hood. He shivered, the narrow slits of his pupils dilating. Salha had told me that, just like a peacock's tail, an Ordosian's hood was a symbol of sexual selection and used to attract females—among other things. The wider the hood, the thicker the brow arch, the greater the number of rings lining it, the more prime the specimen. Szaro was fanning his 'peacock tail' to entice me.

I wrapped my arms around his neck, and he drew me into his embrace. The rattling purr that rose from his throat echoed the soft moan that escaped me at the feel of his hard body against my naked skin. The gentle scraping of the scales on his tail as it moved from side to side to keep us above-water resonated directly between my thighs. His hands roamed my back, one settling on my bum, while the other cupped my nape. I lifted my face, anticipating the kiss that I received moments later.

I melted against him. And for the first time, Szaro's lips parted as he deepened the kiss. I had feared that moment, not knowing how I would respond to his reptilian tongue. It certainly felt strange at first with it being narrower and longer. So, I stopped trying and gave him the lead. His rattling purr expressed his approval and soon our tongues were dancing in tandem. As his hands resumed their exploration, mine began theirs. To my relief, he folded the fins on his upper arms, and I reveled in the soft yet resistant feel of his various scales, from the thicker and wider ones on his shoulders to the smaller, shimmering ones on his chest and arms.

Breaking the kiss, Szaro's lips traced my jawline to my neck, and he bent me backwards so that his mouth could continue its journey on my skin. I instinctively wrapped my legs around his waist, both of my hands hanging on to his muscular upper arms. In this new position, the swaying of his hips to keep us afloat created the most sinful friction of his pelvis against my core. I moaned again from the electric sparks it sent running down my legs and from the burning heat of his mouth sucking on one of my nipples.

Soon he had my inner walls contracting with need. When he pulled me up and reclaimed my mouth, I thought he was going to extrude and lower me onto his length, but he simply slipped his right hand behind my bum and reached around to caress my sex.

My clit was so engorged that a single touch had me moaning loudly against his mouth. Szaro tightened his hold around me, broke the kiss, and stared at my face with an intense look. The movement of his fingers on my little nub was tentative. In my lusty haze, I realized he was unfamiliar with it and was likely studying my reactions to his touch to understand better.

I leaned in to kiss him again, but he moved his head back to continue observing me. Lips parted, breathing loudly as pleasure slowly built within, I closed my eyes and surrendered to his increasingly controlled touch. I threw my head back with a sharp cry when my climax washed over me, my nails digging into Szaro's arms. He emitted that rattling purr again and crushed my lips with a possessive kiss as I continued to tremble against him.

Without stopping, he bent himself backwards until he was lying on his back in the water with me on top of him. Szaro's open hood almost behaved like a flotation device as he resumed swimming along the river. He didn't go back to the shore immediately, circling around in the water as his hands caressed me. I kissed his face and neck while the water licked our feverish skin.

It was only when Szaro turned us around before straightening that I realized he'd finally moved to the shore. With my legs still wrapped around his waist, I let my man carry me to a soft bed of moss a short distance from the water. He laid me down on it, but instead of joining me, he stared at me with an air of wonder, his gaze lingering especially on my legs. I was surprised not to feel embarrassed or extremely self-conscious, but how could I when he looked at me like I was the most beautiful woman in the universe?

He lowered himself and, starting at my feet, traced his fingers up my legs—his lips following in their wake. Goosebumps erupted all over my skin as he reached my knees and rubbed the soft scales of his cheek on my right thigh. A heavy weight seemed to sit on my chest, making it hard to take anything more than shallow breaths as his face inched closer to the apex of my thighs. His broad shoulders nudged my legs apart as he settled between them.

Szaro flicked his tongue and a rattling-purr rose from his throat before his thumb began to gently caress my seam. It then lingered on my clit, which appeared to fascinate him. And then his warm breath fanned over my sex, followed by the burning wetness of his mouth. With a strangled moan, I arched my neck, tilting my head back, one hand pinching my left nipple while the palm of the other rubbed the soft scales of his hood.

My man took his time, exploring, tasting, testing, analyzing each of my responses to his fingers, his tongue, and his mouth on me. The slow build-up of pleasure had an endless string of moans flowing through my lips, my skin tingling with the fire raging within. Through my blissful haze, I saw the tip of his tail curl up near my head, the scales parting to let out his rattles. Heart pounding, I waited for him to begin shaking them, the way he had during our wedding ceremony.

And then he did.

Simultaneously, he stabbed his forked tongue inside of me. Searing heat swept all over my skin, and a blinding light exploded before my eyes under the violence of the orgasm that slammed into me. I couldn't tell what happened for the next few minutes. I was flying way too high. By the time I reconnected with reality—my body still shaking with the last few spasms of ecstasy—Szaro lay on top of me, staring at my face with pride, desire, and possessiveness.

It took me a moment to realize what he was waiting for. I wrapped my arms around his neck and spread my legs wide, allowing him to settle more comfortably between them. His slit-shaped pupils dilated, and his lips parted, giving me a peek of his sharp fangs. And then I felt his scales part below the waist, his stiff, pre-lubricated length resting against my core. He once more paused, his eyes flicking between mine. I nodded, leaving no doubt of my consent.

Szaro smiled and began rubbing himself against me. A powerful shiver ran through me as the 'spikes' along his shaft massaged my clit with each back and forth. After a few such movements, he lowered his head to capture my lips and began to insert himself into me. Good heavens, he was big!

Despite how wet he had made me and his pre-lubrication, my body attempted to resist him. Szaro broke the kiss just long enough to stab his fangs into my neck, injecting me with some of his paralytic venom. It was a small enough quantity that it merely forced my muscles to relax on top of giving me a nice buzz. Seconds later, my body yielded, welcoming him in. Szaro swallowed the voluptuous moan that rose from me, his tongue invading my mouth as his shaft began to move inside of me.

Whatever fantasies I'd entertained since seeing his spikes, reality completely shattered them. When Szaro began to control his spikes, resorbing them on the way in, and expanding them on the way out, I thought I would go insane. With each stroke, a ball of fire exploded in the pit of my stomach, sending liquid flames through my veins, consuming me from within.

Clawing at his scales, shouting with ecstasy, I writhed beneath him as he picked up the pace. Each thrust, deeper, harder, faster, had me tumbling into a vortex of sensations. Szaro wrested another orgasm out of me before slipping his arms behind my knees to open me even wider for him. This time, the controlled, methodical lover that had made me see stars finally seemed to lose control and give in to his own passion.

My head rolled from side to side as he pounded into me, each rocking motion sending electric sparks throughout my body. It was sensory overload. My entire body was nothing more than a maelstrom of overwhelming sensations. From his alien cock wrecking me, to the gentle scraping of his scales against my naked flesh, and to the rattling growl of his moans in my ear, my world narrowed down to Szaro claiming me… destroying me.

When my next climax shattered me, I thought my mind

would fracture. Szaro roared his own release, his seed shooting into my battered insides with powerful spurts. His arms tightening around me in an almost painful embrace kept me rooted in reality. He continued moving in and out of me until his seed was spent. He kissed my face with reverence, whispering words in Ordosian that I couldn't understand. Finally, he turned us around, laying me on top of him and wrapping his arms and tail possessively around my trembling body.

CHAPTER 12
SZARO

With much reluctance, I watched my mate dress, her hair still damp from her morning bath. After joining with her the first time on the shore, I'd claimed her four more times during the night, and once more this morning. Yet still I hungered for her.

I hadn't meant to make her sleep outside, and especially not fully naked. While nights never got cold in this region of Trangor, they were noticeably cooler than the days. My Serena didn't possess the natural protection of scales like we did. Also, unlike her, we were cold-blooded. That meant our bodies could acclimate to the temperature around us, whereas hers would try to maintain a constant temperature. Thankfully, she hadn't seemed to mind or suffer any discomfort from it.

After dressing, Serena fed on rugals. Since she'd compared them to male genitalia, I would never see the fruits the same way. And she was making certain of it, too. Even now, my mate was massaging the fruits with a suggestive expression on her face, touching the tip of her tongue to the mouth of the funnel as if she wanted to lick it, moments before the cream came out. The whole time, her gaze never strayed from mine.

From my research, I knew human males enjoyed being pleasured by their partners taking their penis in their mouth. Serena had not done it to me, although she had wanted to at some point last night. But the need to be inside her had just been too strong. She was so warm, so soft, and the sounds she made as I took her, the way her body trembled beneath me…

Goddess! I felt dizzy just thinking about it.

I didn't know why she had yielded to me last night, and that terrified me. Something had shifted after we slept in the cave. The bond between us had strengthened. And yet, I didn't believe that Serena had renounced her plan to leave once the six months were up.

I can never let her go.

And I would make sure she didn't. Lust wasn't the only reason my mate had joined with me last night. She felt the connection between us. Genuine affection brimmed in her eyes for me. I would fan that flame until it became an all-consuming, raging inferno.

After stealing one last passionate kiss from Serena, I helped her back on Dagas, who had wandered a short distance away while grazing. If nothing else, I took solace in having my female snuggly against me as we shared the Drayshan. The long ride to Tulma flew by in no time.

Thanks to our hunters' efficiency, the threats in the northwest had been eliminated. As Great Hunter of Krada, I'd been derelict in my duties by passing off the role to Mandha and Raskier. But the two males had understood my need for some bonding time with my mate. The first few days of a union usually determined the strength of its foundations. I wanted mine to be indestructible.

However, I only allowed myself the indulgence because I fully trusted my brother and my friend. Mandha's last report on my com indicated that all the remaining Flayer packs that needed to be eliminated were now well within the areas with authorized access for the Federation Hunters. Based on the latest scans, they should be done in a week's time, ten days at the most. I couldn't wait for them to be gone. Their presence was an unwelcome reminder to my mate that she had not chosen me willingly.

She had loved scouting the land and tending the fauna with me yesterday. I wanted that to become Serena's daily routine. I wanted her to discover more of the countless wonders of this world until it became the life *she wanted* and not the one imposed upon her.

As the silhouette of my birth village of Tulma appeared ahead, my mate's delicate scent took on the slightly acrid tinge of fear and anxiety. I did not understand her worry about meeting my parents and other siblings.

A great number of the tribe members greeted our arrival on the square, my family and the Krada hunters among them. I stopped Dagas right before the first stones paving the square, dismounted and helped Serena down. She nervously ran a hand over her plaited hair, and adjusted her hunting suit. The unpleasant familiarity of this scene struck me as I led my mate to the center of the square where the three Elders of Tulma waited below the statue of the Goddess Isshaya. Despite the completely different circumstances that had led us here, my Serena clearly felt on trial again.

Everyone gathered around the square was staring at her. I couldn't fault them for their curiosity. I'd been curious as well the first time I'd laid eyes on Serena, although a certain level of attraction had also factored in. But Tulma had very few interactions with off-worlders, least of all humans. The tribe had never seen a human female in the flesh before, let alone one with golden-brown skin, and least of all a huntress. On top of that, she was the mate of the Great Hunter that a majority of eligible females in Tulma had failed to seduce.

When I'd left the village to seek both a mate and a purpose, many had wondered what kind of female would find grace in my eyes. No one, not even me, could have ever imagined it would be someone like my Serena—my beautiful *Ashina*.

After paying my respects to the Elders and introducing them to my mate, I generally saluted everyone else before approaching my parents. There would be time later to rekindle my friendship with old acquaintances.

"Mother, Father," I said respectfully, pressing my forehead against each of theirs in turn.

"Welcome back, son," my mother said affectionately before turning her golden eyes towards Serena.

"Son," my father said as sole greeting, then he also focused his attention on my mate.

An uneasy feeling settled in the pit of my stomach. Beyond natural curiosity, their gaze lacked the warmth I was used to and that I expected them to express the day I finally brought a mate home.

"This is Serena, my bonded mate," I said, gently caressing her back.

The subtle, but unmistakable hardening in my mother's eyes and stiffening in my father's spine sent all my senses on high alert. My parents didn't approve of my mate. But why? Granted, they would have wanted a pure blood Ordosian female for me, but my happiness mattered to them more. Surely Mandha had told them of the affection my Serena stirred in me. I would have to discover the cause, but not now, not in front of her.

"Serena, these are my parents, my mother Erastra, and my father Leshu," I said in an enthusiastic tone, pretending nothing was amiss.

"It is an honor to meet you Erastra, and you Leshu," Serena said with a nervous laugh.

"We meet you at last, Serena," my father said, barely bowing his head in greeting.

"We've heard much about you," Mother said. "Thank you for

saving my daughter Salha and the little one. Our poor Mandha would have been devastated."

I fought the urge to clench my teeth and barely managed to repress an angry hiss. My parents avoiding my gaze only confirmed the slight had been deliberate, mother underlining it by claiming Mandha's mate as her *daughter* Salha, but both my parents merely referring to my mate as Serena.

"There's no need to thank me," Serena replied. "It was just the right thing to do."

"Mmhmm," my mother replied in a noncommittal fashion.

I then introduced my mate to my three other siblings who had waited off to the side. After exchanging a few words, both of my sisters excused themselves as they had to return to their duties in the atrium, as did my younger brother to head out on a scouting mission. As I intended to spend a couple of days in the village, we would have time to catch up later.

I noticed that Serena was stealing glances at my father. I surmised his imposing size intimidated her. Despite my own great height and broad shoulders, my father was bigger still.

"You've grown some more since I last visited, Father," I said, forcing myself to sound lighthearted.

"I have," Father said with a smug expression.

"And he drove me insane for two weeks with his endless moaning about his molting," Mother said, looking less than impressed.

Serena snorted then tried to hide her laughter in a bout of coughing.

My father turned to glare at my mother. "It was a particularly excruciating one," he said in defensive outrage. "Try having this much old skin to shed and the wretched thing refusing to fall off." He turned back to me. "When you reach my age, you will understand. You are already bigger than I was at your age. By the time you reach mine, I suspect you will be at least three or four centimeters taller and broader."

Serena's eyes widened, and her head jerked towards me. "You're going to grow even bigger than your father?" she asked, flabbergasted.

"More than likely, yes," I said smugly. "Why do you think we molt? Ordosians continue to grow throughout their lives, males faster than females. Our current skin grows too small to contain us, so we shed it to enjoy a new, more comfortable one for a while."

My mate gaped at me, then her gaze slowly roamed over me. By the look on her face, I suspected she was trying to imagine me the size of my father. Her gaze reached my pelvis, paused there for a split second, then she abruptly lifted her head. Serena's overly expressive features failed to hide her sudden embarrassment. I knew then beyond the shadow of a doubt that she'd wondered if my penis scaled up with the rest of me.

Of course, it does.

With a will of its own, my tongue flicked out almost at the same time those of my parents did. To my poor mate's dismay, they had also guessed the cause of her reaction. The taste of Serena's blossoming arousal echoed directly in my nether region, making me instantly ache to extrude. But it was the troubled expression on my parents' faces as they perceived my mate's physical response to me that caught my attention.

They are surprised she's attracted to me.

"I really wish you guys wouldn't do that," Serena mumbled under her breath, mortified.

I laughed, feeling a sliver of sympathy for her. Having my scent betray countless things about me to others was a fact of life. I grew up being subjected to it and doing it to others. It had to be unnerving for someone like her who'd never experienced it before.

"Will you stay a while or are you only passing through?" my mother asked.

"If it is no trouble, Mandha, my mate, and I intend to spend a couple of days with you," I said carefully. "It will be a chance for Serena to discover where we grew up and to get to know her new family. The Flayer situation is under control. Raskier will take our hunters back to Krada so the village doesn't remain too long with a reduced number of defenders."

In light of their lukewarm reception to my mate, I'd expected my parents to balk at that prospect, but my mother's enthusiastic reaction at the news immediately made me suspicious. She was up to something and would use our stay to bring her plans to fruition, whatever they were. I needed to find a private moment with my parents to confront them about their attitude.

"Well then, I will take Serena to your old room, give her a tour of the house, and get to know her while you catch up with your father and sort out the return of your hunters," my mother said in a tone that brooked no argument.

"But—"

"We do have much to discuss," my father said, interrupting me. "Leave the females to their own devices."

My stomach knotted with apprehension as I turned to look at Serena. I didn't want to leave her alone with my mother until I had a better sense of what had prompted her odd behavior. My mother had always been a warm, loving, and supportive female.

"It's okay," Serena said, caressing my chest in a soothing gesture. "This will be my chance to get your mother to reveal all of your shameful childhood secrets."

Mother snorted. "It will take far more than a couple of days for that. Come, Serena."

My eyes locked with my mother's as she was gesturing for my mate to follow her. She held my warning gaze defiantly. I watched them depart, worry gnawing at me. I turned back to glare at my father.

"What's going on? Why did you and mother disrespect my mate?" I hissed.

"Disrespect?" my father asked, tilting his head to the side

and looking at me as if I'd said something ludicrous. "You think *we* disrespected *her*? Tell me, Son, did you notice how the tribe looked at the two of you when you arrived?"

I shrugged. "A rather rude curiosity that put my mate ill at ease."

"It's only curiosity that you saw? Or is that all you *chose* to see?" he retorted, his gaze boring into mine with the stern demeanor he used to display in my youth when I wouldn't take my training seriously.

"What else was I supposed to see?"

"Pity," he said with a cold voice.

I recoiled, feeling like I'd just received a punch in the gut. A million thoughts swirled in my mind as I replayed in my head the looks the tribe had indeed cast on my mate and me. My hands fisted, my fangs descended, and my venom glands swelled as anger surged within me. They had looked on *her* with curiosity laced with disdain. They had looked on *me* with disappointment and pity.

"Pity?" I hissed, advancing menacingly towards my father. "Pity for what? Because I bonded with an off-worlder?"

"Do not bare your fangs at me, Szaro Kota," my father snapped, his impressive hood widening further in a sign of dominance, while his muscles bulged under his scales. "I'll rip them right out of your mouth to teach you respect."

I swallowed painfully past my overflowing glands, closed my mouth, and bowed my head in submission. I'd never disrespected my sire before.

But then, I'd never had a mate for him to disrespect either.

"We do not care that you chose an off-worlder for your mate," my father continued, his voice still clipped but his anger mollified by my show of submission. "But you are Szaro Kota, son of Leshu, and Great Hunter of Krada. Half the females of Tulma had hoped to bear your offspring, whether as your life companion or as your bonded mate. You refused them all to shackle yourself in this farce of a union!"

"It is not a farce!" I shouted, not caring who heard our argument. "Serena and I were bound before the Goddess and the tribe of Krada. I demand respect for my mate!"

"She is *not* your mate. *You* bound your life to Serena before the Goddess and all of Krada. *She* did not."

I felt my blood drain from my face as understanding finally dawned on me. "We addressed the matter with Elder Krathi. She agreed—"

"Elder Krathi is a fool," my father interrupted angrily. "She and your adoptive tribe may have found it acceptable, but she should have known the other tribes would not. The word has spread far and wide. And what do you think everyone is saying?"

I swallowed down the bile rising in my throat. I didn't care what others thought of me, but I couldn't accept that they thought ill of my mate, or that my situation brought shame to my family.

"I will not have my firstborn son be made a mockery," my father added, lifting his chin. "Nor will your mother. I can assure you that she will see this resolved before you depart."

I nodded stiffly.

CHAPTER 13
SERENA

I tried to silence my nerves as I followed Erastra into their dwelling. Unlike Krada, the Tulma village wasn't enclosed by a mountain, but surrounded by water. We crossed a wide bridge to the diamond-shaped island. Most of the residences were waterfront properties. Built mainly of stone and wood, they all possessed immense reflective windows that prevented people outside from spying on the residents within.

As with Szaro's home, his father's dwelling clearly established his status in the Tulma tribe. It was massive and highly ornate on the outside. Delicate patterns had been carved in bas-relief on both the stone and wood shaping the building. I'd seen similar carvings in Krada. But there, like here, not many dwellings had them. Life companions didn't sculpt their façade, only bonded mates. The extent and complexity of the decorations revealed how long a married couple had occupied the house. It was the male's homage to his wife. For each year of their union, each birth of a child, and any great event related to their family, more sculpting went up on the wall.

I knew Szaro wanted to start sculpting the façade of his cave in Krada. According to Salha, my first meeting with Szaro by the border, then me rescuing her and Eicu would be the first things going up in a stylized fashion. But before I could dwell on how I felt about it, Erastra opened the door to the house and ushered me in. My jaw dropped at the beauty that greeted me inside.

As I'd come to expect in an Ordosian dwelling, 'comfort' furniture was scarce. No couches, chairs, or cushiony surfaces, nothing that would traditionally translate as a living room or dining room. And yet, the large room we entered into qualified as both. On one side, a massive table with exquisitely sculpted edges and legs sat in front of a series of shelves that were just as ornate. Some boxes that looked like board games were shelved there. On the other side, a number of circular heating plates surrounded a low table in a half-circle. And a wall-mounted giant screen hung in front of them.

But what held my attention were the immense statues of an Ordosian female at each end of the room, each one framed by massive windows. They acted almost like a column, their hoods touching the ceiling as their beautiful faces looked down into the room, and only the tips of their tails touching the floor. Arms spread wide, they held the ribbons the females had danced with during our wedding. In this sculpted version, the ribbons ran along the ceiling like crown moldings.

Speechless, I followed Erastra as she took me to Szaro's old room. That, too, stunned me. Where his room in his own dwelling had been completely bare, the walls of this one were decorated with weapons, bones, scales, and dried plants or branches, each of them linked by a pattern carved on the wall. It took me less than a second to realize this was his journey as a hunter—from the child-sized wooden practice bow, to the fearsome skull of a creature I'd never seen before.

"As is his duty, Leshu records the history of each of our offspring," Erastra said proudly as she gazed at the wall. She went to the last object at the end of the sculpted thread. It looked like the head of a spear made of stone. "My mate made this to mark the day Szaro became the Great Hunter of Krada—the rock mountain village. Leshu is eager to prolong the thread. But since Szaro refuses to sire an offspring with a life companion, the next addition to this wall will likely be to mark his bonding."

The uneasy feeling that had been gnawing at me since I first entered the village, which had intensified the moment I met Szaro's parents, only went up another notch.

"If he's so eager, why hasn't he started yet?" I challenged.

Erastra turned to face me, a hard glimmer in her golden eyes as she stared at me defiantly. "Because there's nothing to add. Szaro isn't bonded."

A part of me had known this was coming, but it still felt like a slap in the face. I clenched my teeth and took a deep breath to keep my cool. I held her gaze unwaveringly, refusing to be bullied.

"You really don't like me much, do you?" I said in a clipped tone.

"I do not dislike you," Erastra refuted, in a casual tone. "Or rather, I *no longer* dislike you since meeting you. But I have yet to decide if I like you."

"You don't dislike me? Yet you and everyone else in the village looked at me with contempt the minute we arrived. And now you insult Szaro and me by dismissing our bond like it doesn't exist?" I snapped.

"Because it doesn't!" she hissed, before advancing towards me. It felt menacing, but she remained at a respectable distance, although I'd be unable to escape if she decided to attack.

"It sure as hell does!" I said, keeping my voice barely below a shout. "Szaro and I were married twice. First according to human laws, and then through an elaborate Ordosian ritual. We were bound before all of Krada and your Goddess."

"Szaro bound himself to *you. You* did not bind to *him*!" Erastra shouted, anger twisting her pretty features.

I recoiled, utterly confused. I replayed the ceremony in my head, trying to figure out what I had failed to accomplish.

"What… what do you mean? I did everything that I was told to do. I stood in the middle of the circle, Szaro and I embraced each other, the females danced around us, then the Elders made that circle, and we kissed. What more was I supposed to do?"

"Szaro danced for you. Did *you* dance for him?"

I shook my head, frowning. "No. Salha danced in my stead since I didn't know the choreography."

"Salha is *not* his mate! She cannot bind him," Erastra grumbled. "Why would you let another female perform the most important act of your life?"

"Look, you need to get the hell off my back," I snapped, starting to lose patience. "In case you haven't noticed, I'm not Ordosian." I gestured at myself. "I don't know your goddamn rituals because they are not documented anywhere. I was told to go to the circle, sit my ass down, and wait until someone gave me more instructions. I didn't even know there was supposed to be any kind of freaking dancing involved. If it was so damn important, then someone should have told me. Don't give me shit because I can't read minds!"

I inhaled deeply and slowly breathed out, closing my eyes to try and regain control. As much as venting my frustration had been liberating, I felt horrible for raising my voice at Szaro's mom. Whatever our current issues, she was my mother-in-law. To my surprise, instead of escalating things, my outburst seemed to dampen some of Erastra's anger. She pursed her lips and gave me an assessing look before nodding stiffly.

"You make a valid point," Erastra conceded. "And Elder Krathi will hear of my wrath for allowing this humiliation to befall my son. You were already in the village. They could have delayed the ceremony by a few days to allow you to learn how to handle the bands so that the bond could be done properly. The choreography doesn't have to be perfect."

"Hold on! Back up! What do you mean *this humiliation*?" I demanded.

Erastra looked at me. This time, anger gave way to pain and shame. "The fact that you didn't dance for him told the whole world that you are willing to take advantage of all the benefits of having a bonded mate, but that you are not ready to reciprocate because you do not deem him worthy of you."

Shocked, I covered my mouth with my hand while staring at her in disbelief.

"My son was the most sought-after male here and in every village he's visited. But no female ever met his approval," Erastra said in a voice filled with pain. "And now the word is spreading that he chose an off-worlder only to be the one found lacking. He's become a mockery."

"That's bullshit!" I hissed. "If they knew people would react that way, why the hell did Elder Krathi—and Szaro for that matter—allow it?"

"Because Krada prides itself on being 'progressive' in its ways and adaptive to ever changing situations," Erastra said with irritation while waving a dismissive hand. "That is why most of the interactions with your Federation have been handled through them. But they forget they do not live in isolation. The other tribes still observe the old ways, and things that happen have consequences."

"Okay, fine. But crying over spilled milk isn't going to change anything," I said, pissed beyond words that anyone would mock Szaro, and especially not over a miscommunication. I wanted to go out and shoot one of my bolts in the tail of any asshole who looked at my man the wrong way. "How do we fix this?"

"You must dance for him," Erastra said forcefully.

"All right. Let's do it," I said.

Erastra recoiled, and her eyes widened in shock. "You… you will do it?"

"Of course!" I replied as if it was self-evident—because it was. "Why would you even doubt that? Szaro saved my life and has been nothing but wonderful to me from day one. I will *not* be the reason anyone humiliates him. He does not deserve this."

Her face softened, and her eyes brimmed with gratitude. "You have affection for him," she said with a sliver of surprise in her voice.

My face heated. "He's a good man. Well, a good male."

"Thank you, daughter," Erastra replied. "We are very proud of him."

Her acknowledging me as a daughter moved me deeply. I wasn't very close to my mother, but I still loved and missed her.

"So, what do we do now? Can you teach me the choreography?" I asked shyly.

"The choreography isn't important," Erastra said dismissively. "The bands are what matter. You can dance however you want. Anyway, your anatomy isn't suited for our choreographies. How you move the bands is what counts. For that, too, there is no specific shape or pattern to create. It's just the complexity that marks the extent of your commitment to the bond, and the fluidity that expresses the happiness and success of your union. You are the bond that ties your family unit. The bands are but an extension of you. Come, I will show you."

We went back to the living area where she reached for an ornate wooden box on a shelf. It contained the neatly folded pair of ribbons she called bands. She picked one up and handed it to me.

"These are my bonding bands," Erastra said in a wistful voice. "You can train with them while we get a pair especially made for you. It will only take a few hours, so they will be ready in time for you to perform the dance tomorrow."

I frowned at the weight of the single band she had given me. "This is heavy," I said with worry. It weighed at least 10 pounds. "I will not be able to dance more than a few seconds while swirling the band around with this weight on each arm. I will tire too quickly."

Erastra's jaw dropped. She stared at my arms for a moment, as if she could see my muscles through my hunting suit, then looked back at my face, her mind racing.

"The fabric the bands are made of is actually quite light. The seamstress applies a substance onto it to make it heavier, and for it to not fold in on itself," Erastra said pensively. "We can ask her to make yours lighter, but it might impede your ability to make them work as intended."

I chewed my bottom lip.

"There might be an alternative," I said cautiously. Erastra tilted her head with curiosity. "A few years back, I used to perform a dance with a ribbon, for which I had trained intensively. I was ranked among the most skillful dancers of Earth at the time in a planet-wide sports competition we call the Olympics. The dance uses a ribbon… a band like this, but narrower, and attached to a stick," I said nervously. "If the choreography doesn't matter, only how we manipulate the band, would it be okay for me to do that? Since we need to create a set of bands for me, maybe we could create the ribbon wand for me instead?"

Erastra hesitated, eyeing me with an uncertain expression. "And that dance involves complex movements of the band?" she asked.

I nodded vigorously. "Yes. Do you have a tablet I can borrow? I should be able to find images online."

Sure enough, moments after she gave me a tablet, I quickly found a few pictures and videos that instantly reassured my mother-in-law.

"They are much narrower than the bands, but this seems like an acceptable compromise," Erastra said. "Do you know the measurements?"

"Yes," I said, excitement bubbling inside of me.

It had been more than seven years since I'd stopped rhythmic gymnastics at a competitive level—or had any further training, for that matter. But I still performed it from time to time just for fun, and my regular yoga meditation had kept me toned and flexible. This I could do with confidence. Part of me also looked forward to performing in front of an audience again.

Erastra took me to the seamstress, whose cool demeanor instantly warmed once my mother-in-law explained the purpose of our visit. She was shocked at first by my request for the ribbon wand instead of the bands. For a moment, I feared straying from their custom again would not only defeat the purpose of this dance, but also further alienate the Ordosians where my bond with Szaro was concerned. However, showing her the pictures of the gymnast fully mollified her.

"You can make this narrow band swirl like in these images?" she asked.

"More even," I said smugly. "But only if I get a good wand."

The impressed expression on her face tickled me pink. But seeing Erastra lift her chin proudly touched me even more. In that instant, I knew I would perform my ass off on that circle, not only to restore Szaro's honor, but to vindicate my mother-in-law for the humiliation she and her family had endured over this misunderstanding.

"Then it will be a dance to remember," the seamstress said. "I will start working on it right away. You will be pleased with the final result."

I thanked the female and let Erastra lead me back outside. She then proceeded to give me a tour of the village with a stop in their atrium for me to gather something to eat. When we returned to her dwelling, she took me to the back of the house, onto the terrace I had not seen yet. The view took my breath away. While I still preferred the hidden valley behind Szaro's house, this was amazing.

At least twenty meters by ten, the stone terrace appeared to be floating in the ocean. The edge served as a springboard to dive into the water. A small ramp on the side allowed the Ordosians to climb back up. In the left corner, a circular hole with elevated edges to avoid someone inadvertently falling in, held a series of live shrimp-like critters that had gotten trapped inside. A table stood a couple of meters away from it, including —to my great surprise—a cushioned bench, perfect for a human to sit on. And next to it, a cooking stone. I instantly knew that Mandha had warned his parents of my specific needs before our arrival.

But it was the large fish jumping out of the water that blew my mind. From a distance they looked like a cross between a dolphin and a betta fish.

"Later, Szaro will take you to swim with them if you like," Erastra said in a friendly tone, while bringing the cooking stone to the table. "But now, eat. I will not have my son accuse me of starving his female."

I settled at the table and ate my fruits and veggies, while Erastra shelled the 'shrimps' and put them to cook on the stone for me. By the time Szaro and his father finally returned home, his mother had told me every single one of his embarrassing childhood stories.

CHAPTER 14
SZARO

I stood nervously at the edge of the circle, bare but for the golden necklace with the bloodstone of my forefathers, since all of my adornments were back in Krada. All of Tulma sat behind me in this unusual ceremony to complete my partial bond. I had agonized about having Serena sit out the dance during our original ceremony, but I knew she didn't have the physical strength to hold the bands.

I had convinced myself that our bond wouldn't be contested even though she hadn't danced. Finding out that every other tribe challenged it had felt like a shower of acid. Serena was my mate. Our joining by the river had only confirmed there would never be another female for me. Therefore, I was beyond grateful to my mother for setting all of this in motion. It would erase any doubt that my Serena had meant to claim me during the first ceremony.

Although we wouldn't perform the full ritual tonight, Serena and I still showered beforehand. My chest warmed remembering her squeal of delight on our first day in Tulma when I showed the private shower and toilet I had Mandha and my father prepare for her before our arrival. It was makeshift, quickly put together to be functional. But in the future, I intended to have every tribe set a permanent one for the times my mate and I would visit them.

No female dancers surrounded the circle, no males would beat their drums, and no warrior would challenge me tonight. But our three Elders stood on the dais at the feet of the Goddess overlooking the circle which, for tonight only, had been covered with a thin mat to pad the hard stone floor.

My heart leapt in my chest, and a hush fell over the audience when the delicate figure of my mate approached from the left side of the circle and walked all the way to the center. She was wearing what I had come to call her underwear. They were in fact called a sports bra and training shorts. Both were black and hid very little of her beautiful skin. I wished she would dress that lightly more often. To my surprise, Serena was barefoot, aside from some kind of black strips of fabric wrapped around her ankles and her toes. In her hand, she held the narrow band on a stick.

She kneeled facing me, her gaze locking with mine. A silent communication passed between us. The confidence in her eyes partially appeased the worry that had been gnawing at me. Serena smiled then cast a glance at Mandha. My mate nodded with a subtle movement, giving my brother the signal to start the off-worlder music she had selected.

Serena bowed, her forehead pressed to the mat and both her arms extended in front of her. I held my breath, as the silence stretched for a few more seconds. Then the clear notes of a peaceful melody rose around us. Still in her bowed position, Serena began flicking the stick, just above the ground. The band appeared to be slithering at high speed in front of her while her free arm undulated in a graceful movement. She suddenly sat up, swirling the ribbon in wide movements all around her, a luminous smile lighting up her face.

A collective gasp of awe rose from the crowd. Our bands

were too big and heavy to perform the complex and rapid movements of my mate's ribbon. And the glowing, light-blue fabric of the ribbon in the darkness made it look like a spirit serpent was cavorting in a joyous dance around her.

Without stopping the movement of the ribbon, Serena threw her free hand back, pushing up to her toes, and flipping backward using her hand as leverage, to end up in a standing position. She then started running around the circle, performing impossible dance steps, jumps, and acrobatic movements—some of which made me fear she'd injure herself—while her ribbon drew the most mesmerizing arabesque. Watching her stand on the tip of one foot and spin around impressed me. But seeing her raise her second leg so the toes of that foot would point at the sky without losing her balance and swirling her ribbon in a frenzy took my breath away. I was feeling choked with emotions, an indescribable pride filling my heart.

And then disaster…

I watched in horror as, after pivoting a few times on herself, Serena threw her stick. My heart shattered, and my blood turned to acid as horrified gasps rose behind me. Time seemed to slow down as Serena performed a few tumbles and a twirl, then blindly caught the stick, flowing into more patterns with the ribbon.

"She caught it…" I whispered in shock and disbelief.

Just as the words left my mouth, a collective roar rose behind me followed by the sound of countless rattles honoring my mate. I felt faint as I stared at Serena's riveting performance. She was moving faster, in tandem with the music that had become more intense, more dramatic. Twice more my female threw the ribbon, and twice more she caught it before it ever touched the floor. Both times, she barely had to look to do so—her heart knew where it would be.

No matter what challenges came our way, no matter who or

what tried to tear us apart, she would always catch us and keep our bond flowing towards our joint future.

As the music began to slow down, Serena came back to the center of the circle and gestured for me to come. My heart overflowed with pride and too many emotions to give them a name as I went to her. My mate circled around me a few times, her ribbon swirling in complex patterns, erasing any doubt that I'd been properly claimed and bound. The music came to a stop at the same time my female did right in front of me. I pulled her into my embrace and crushed her lips in a possessive kiss while my tail wrapped around her.

I could barely hear the rattling saluting us, or even the Elders giving their blessing as they surrounded us with their hands linked. When they parted, I didn't stay for the congratulations and accolades of my birth tribe. All I could see, all that I cared about, was the beautiful goddess in my arms. Eyes locked with Serena, I picked her up, and she wrapped her legs around my waist. Without a word, I took her to my parents' dwelling under the cheers of the crowd.

After what felt like an eternity, we entered the house, and I took Serena directly to my room. I was already removing her clothes—almost ripping them off—before the door was fully closed behind me. Last night, Serena had felt self-conscious about joining with me, as she'd feared my parents and siblings would hear us. Despite my reassurances about the soundproof walls, she still insisted that we keep it quiet. To please her, I had complied. Tonight, I didn't care if they could hear us all the way up in the orbiting docking station of the Federation. I was a properly bonded male about to claim his goddess of a mate.

Although my parents had brought in an improvised mattress for Serena last night, she had slept on top of me. But we had first made love on the mattress, as we would now to protect her from the hard floor.

I tossed her top to the floor and claimed her lips in a greedy kiss. Even as I lowered her onto the cushion, my tongue invaded her mouth. It had been so strange the first time we had kissed that way. I hadn't even been certain that I would ever get used to the odd shape and size of her tongue or the rows of blunt teeth that filled her mouth instead of the handful of sharp ones in ours. But now I couldn't get enough of kissing her. I couldn't get enough of her, period.

And right now, a different taste called to me and made my blood boil with need. Reluctantly breaking the kiss, I brushed my lips down her neck to her chest. Unable to resist, I stopped at the hardening bud of her breast, my tongue teasing the dark brown circle of her areola before I sucked on her nipple. I loved the slightly salty taste of her skin owing to her previous exertion.

Although my mate lifted her chest for greater friction and placed a hand at the back of my head as if to keep me in place, I resumed my journey down to my prize. Serena's stomach quivered as I nipped at her navel. Hooking my fingers in the waist of her shorts, I pulled them down while licking and sucking on the sensitive flesh of her pelvis. A shiver ran through her, making me purr with approval. I loved how responsive my mate was to my touch.

My only disappointment as I removed her bottom garment, was the absence of little curls around her slit. My research had indicated that humans had some there and under their armpits. Some of them even had them on their legs and most every other part of their bodies—especially the males. But Serena had informed me that she'd never had leg hair—which wasn't uncommon for human females of her ethnicity—and that she had permanently removed the ones under her arms and around her sex so she would never have to deal with them anymore. A pity. I would have loved to know if they were as soft as the tight curls of her long hair.

To my shock, just as I was about to sate my hunger, Serena

pressed her palm to my forehead and pushed me back. My head jerked up, and I cast a questioning look at her.

"Lie down," she said, her golden eyes darkened by desire.

"But, I want—"

"Oh, you will. Just lie down. Trust me."

Confused, I considered resisting but complied.

"Extrude," she commanded.

"But—"

"Stop arguing," Serena said with a frown. "I also want to taste you. We can both do it at the same time."

My eyes widened, and a ball of lust exploded in my pelvic area, making me growl with need. I had fantasized about this from the first time I'd researched human couplings. I extruded with an almost painful groan as my female straddled me, carefully aligning her core with my face. Without any preliminaries, I dove right in and stuck my tongue inside of her. Serena shivered, and I gripped the fleshy curve on her behind with both hands to keep her in place as I feasted.

But it soon proved challenging as my mate's delicate hand closed around my length and began to stroke me. The wet heat of her tongue licking my shaft, teasing my spikes, and circling around the head had me moaning as liquid fire bubbled in the pit of my stomach. When she finally took me in her mouth, I nearly spilled. Serena's hand squeezed and stroked the base of my penis in counterpoint to the movement of her head bobbing over me. My abdominal muscles constricted painfully as I battled to rein myself in. I couldn't find my release before my mate.

Slipping one hand between my female's thighs, I rubbed her little nub while accelerating the speed and strength of my tongue making love to her. I especially focused on the little bundle of nerves inside her that always had her toppling over the edge of bliss in no time. Fearing I might still lose the battle, I raised my tail near Serena's ear, extruded my rattles, and produced the mating sound that acted like a powerful aphrodisiac.

Within seconds, my mate cried out, throwing her head back in ecstasy. This reprieve allowed me to regain partial control. As she rode the waves of pleasure, I slipped out from under her, holding her still on all fours as I positioned myself behind her. That, too, I had fantasized about. It was impossible to join with Ordosian females that way. I pushed myself inside my mate, the searing heat of her tight sheath closing all around me.

I hissed with pleasure, my spikes aching to kick into action. I silenced the urge, giving my mate time to adjust to my girth as I slowly pumped in and out of her. There was something raw and primal about holding my female like this as she submitted to my possession. Serena moaned, and her back arched as she began to rock back and forth in counterpoint to my own movements. Holding her hip with one hand, I caressed her back with the other, letting my claws out to gently scrape her skin.

Serena emitted a strangled cry and turned to look at me over her shoulder. The look of pure lust she gave me echoed straight in my groin. She licked her lips in such a lascivious fashion, the memory of the way it felt swirling around my length when she pleasured me with her mouth slammed into me with dizzying violence. Something snapped inside me. Holding her hips with both hands, my claws digging a bit too forcefully into her tender flesh, I started pounding into her. Serena threw her head back and shouted out with bliss.

On instinct, I leaned forward, slipped my left arm in front of her chest, and lifted her while still thrusting frantically into her. Still kneeling, her back against my chest, Serena twisted to look back at me. I captured her lips in a passionate kiss. My right hand reached for her clitoris, and I allowed my spikes to undulate inside of her.

My mate instantly went off. I swallowed the shout of her climax and tightened my hold around her as spasms of ecstasy rocked her. Like with every time she found release, my mate's inner walls clamped down on my penis, trying to force my orgasm out of me. I resisted and pursued my attentions until my mate came down from her high.

I released her only long enough to lay her back on the mattress before burying myself deep inside of her again. This time, my gaze never left my mate's beautiful face as I plowed into her. Goddess, I would never tire of the way Serena looked, her face dissolved in an expression of pure bliss, the way she writhed beneath me—her pelvis gyrating as she met me thrust for thrust, her throaty voice spurring me on, chanting my name, and begging for more—to take her deeper, harder.

I never saw her climax coming. It swept her away so suddenly, I got caught in the tidal wave. I cried out, my seed shooting into my woman with such strength it left me dizzy. My loins were on fire. Each spurt another shot of liquid ecstasy pouring from me. I hadn't meant to lock with my mate. The head of my penis swelled, sealing my seed inside Serena to increase the chances of conception. At the same time, I felt my mating hormone sac empty itself, sending another shiver of bliss down my spine as it poured into my female. It would attempt to regulate Serena's hormonal levels to facilitate conception.

It was a pointless endeavor at this time. My female wasn't in her fertile period—her scent told me as much. Even though I hadn't intended to do this, I reveled in the connection. I turned us around, cradling my trembling mate in my arms. How I loved the feel of her like this, her body slick with sweat, thrumming from the pleasure I'd given her, clinging to me as if she wished we could be even closer, fused as one body and soul. She seemed so fragile, so vulnerable, and so trusting in her abandon.

I gently caressed her damp hair as she sighed with content, her head resting on my chest. I tightened my embrace, my heart filling with affection and longing as pictures of my mate swelling with our offspring danced before my mind's eye.

I closed my eyes and fell asleep wearing a wistful smile.

CHAPTER 15

SERENA

We ended up extending our stay in Tulma by another couple of days. If I had my way, we probably would have stuck around even longer. Leshu and Erastra were a freaking riot. At first I'd feared their relationship had soured over the years the way she was always on his ass and criticizing one thing or another that he did, like she had with his molting. But then I realized it was a game between them. When she had nothing to give him a hard time about, he would deliberately do something to egg her on. Many times, I caught one or the other trying to hide their face so we wouldn't see the laughter they couldn't suppress.

But whenever they weren't picking on each other, they would cuddle in the sweetest way. It made me ache with longing. Going to the shower and seeing that beast of a male gently scraping the scales of the hood, back, and tail of Erastra with the porous stone they used to wash had me melting from the inside out.

Knowing that Szaro would grow to be as big or bigger than his sire messed with my head big time. There was something irresistible about an intimidating mountain of a male who turned into a teddy bear for his one and only. Szaro's siblings were also a lot of fun, but their mother remained the one I had truly bonded with.

To my shock, my dancing ribbon became an overnight sensation. The poor seamstress got swamped with requests—the Ordosian females wanting them in pairs, like their bands. Catching a few females practicing with them gave me warm fuzzies.

Returning home was bittersweet, but Erastra made me promise to come visit often. As Krada's Great Hunter, Szaro couldn't stay away any longer. Elder Krathi only cut him some slack because I claimed it was our honeymoon—which they didn't have here.

Upon our return, I nearly fell on my ass when I saw the work Irco had done in our absence. The cooking area outside the house could have been the outdoor kitchen of a fancy mansion, complete with a sink and cooling unit. The dining room set inside the main room had turned out even more beautiful than the reference I had provided the builder. My bed was to die for, and the mattress felt like sleeping on a cloud. It almost made me want to reconsider sleeping on top of Szaro. Almost…

That didn't mean we wouldn't use it to play naughty.

But what truly took my breath away was the in-house hygiene room my lovable wretch of a husband had secretly authorized behind my back. Irco had noticed my reaction to a crazy luxury bathroom while we were looking for references for my toilet and shower in the shared cleansing area. I couldn't believe he'd shown it to Szaro and they'd plotted this. I couldn't get mad. I loved it. It was beyond beautiful. But Szaro's determination to give me a good life and make me happy was doing quite a number on me.

I expected guilt to gnaw at me, seeing my husband shaping his house to accommodate a wife he wasn't even certain would stay. But it was nowhere to be found. On a subconscious level, I already knew the chances of me leaving Trangor—of leaving

Szaro—were dwindling with each passing day. I was falling hard and fast for that Naga. But I was also falling for this world, these people, and this lifestyle…

The next twelve days went by peacefully. With no more Flayer incursions near vulnerable sectors, we let the Federation hunters finish the task for which they'd been brought here. In two, three more days at the most, they would pack up and leave. My chest didn't constrict with sorrow, and no distress or sense of doom claimed me. Just peace. During the past couple of weeks, I'd fallen into a nice routine with the hunters as we went out scouting and tending to the local flora and fauna. There was always something to do, something new to discover.

I finished cooking my meal and went to set the table on the terrace, as had become the norm for us. Szaro was late. He usually sat with me, keeping me company because he knew eating was a social thing for humans. And even though he couldn't share my meals with me, he nonetheless wanted to give me that sense of companionship.

Just as that thought was crossing my mind, the front door opened, and Szaro came gliding in, carrying a big bowl. He gestured for me to wait a minute and went into the kitchen. I waited patiently, my curiosity piqued. He came out to the terrace carrying a plate filled with cubes. He placed it on the table across from me. It took me a moment to recognize it as raw meat… complete with fur and claws. My eyes widened, and I stared questioningly at Szaro.

"I have depleted my reserves," he explained, gesturing for me to take a seat. "From now on, I will share dinner with you."

My jaw dropped as I stared at his less than appetizing plate of food. I looked up at his smiling face, and I just melted again. Damn the man and his countless attentions.

"That's super sweet. But that doesn't seem anywhere near enough food for you," I said, worried.

"It should last me a day, maybe less," Szaro said with a

shrug. "But I would rather err on the side of caution. It has been a while since I've not eaten to last me at least a few weeks."

"You're really awesome," I said with affection.

"I know," he said smugly.

I huffed and scrunched my face at him. "I take it back."

"You can't. You've already said it, and you absolutely meant it," he retorted with an obnoxious grin that made me want to throw something at him.

In that instant, I saw the Leshu he would become, and I melted some more. He'd brought a fork—which I knew the Ordosians didn't use—and stabbed a piece of meat before shoving it into his mouth.

He didn't chew.

It freaked me out a little, but nowhere near as much as I'd feared. Then again, his throat barely swelled as the piece went down. Although they weren't, snakes always looked like they were in agony as their faces stretched to impossible extents to let the food in.

"You cut it up in small pieces for me," I whispered, understanding dawning on me.

Szaro smiled but remained silent for a few more seconds until the piece cleared his throat.

"I would normally swallow this creature whole," he conceded. "But I'm pretty certain you would not have enjoyed the spectacle while trying to eat."

I squirmed on my chair, embarrassment heating my cheeks. "It is the way of your people," I said, sounding a little on the defensive. "It would distress me at first, but I'd eventually get over it."

"Why distress you when there is a simple alternative that really doesn't make much of a difference for me?" he challenged. "Whether I swallow multiple smaller pieces, or a single large one, it will take me approximately the same time. The only difference is that one allows me to keep you company and have a conversation, whereas the other pretty much puts me out of commission for the duration."

I made a face at him, which made him chuckle. "When you put it that way, it's hard to argue," I mumbled.

He grinned, stabbed another piece—this one included fur—and shoved it into his mouth. Thankfully, my gag reflex didn't kick in. This would still take some getting used to. I took a couple more bites of my own dish when a sudden thought hit me as I remembered my conversation with Salha.

"So… the pieces you've eaten so far had bones in them, and this one has fur," I said, choosing my words carefully. "Snakes can digest bones, but not fur, feathers, horns, or anything that contains keratin. Are you going to turn that fur into a 'furball' type of thing and just spit it out?"

Szaro chuckled, no doubt in reaction to the expression on my face. I'd tried to keep it neutral, but…

"Actually, the first piece I ate had bones and teeth, and the second one had fur, bones, and claws," Szaro specified with an amused expression.

I stared at him in horror, and my right eye twitched. Szaro threw his head back and burst out laughing. It was deep and powerful, his shoulders shaking with mirth. Under different circumstances, I'd be gushing over how handsome and badass he looked, but I was a little too busy being traumatized.

"And yes, I will spit out a 'furball' type of thing to get rid of the fur and claws. But have no fear, I will spare you that spectacle," he continued, amusement still sparkling in his eyes. "And no, it won't happen in the next minute or so. It will take a couple of hours for the process to complete."

"Right," I mumbled. "You're having way too much fun with that."

"I am, my mate. I am," he confessed without the slightest remorse.

Even though some of his ways and biological functions

freaked me out, I could get over them… once I recovered from the culture shock. But I loved that I could discuss it with Szaro, and he didn't get offended by my involuntary responses. My wretched face was overly expressive and diplomatically challenged.

We finished eating while chatting away amicably. However gross I found his food, I had actually enjoyed sharing a meal, instead of him just keeping me company while I stuffed my face. Once again, my heart warmed for Szaro's constant thoughtfulness.

As was his wont, my dear husband picked up the dirty dishes so that he could wash them. Before heading back inside, he leaned forward to kiss me. I recoiled, and slapped my palm on his chest to hold him back.

"Hell no!" I said in response to his stunned expression. "You are *not* kissing me with that mouth, not after the freaky stuff that just went into it. Go use my mouthwash first, then I'll reconsider."

Szaro's eyes bulged so much, they looked on the verge of popping out of his head. "What?" he exclaimed, flabbergasted. "You eat dead stuff all the time and never have a problem kissing me."

"That is definitely not the same thing," I said, shocked he would compare the two. "You just ate teeth, fur, and claws!"

"Technically, I swallowed them along with the meat they were attached to. And you just ate a kweelzy's butt and feet. How is that better?"

"It's called ham and hock," I argued. "AND it's cooked, eliminating all the nasty stuff."

"Those are just fancy terms to describe an animal's ass and feet," Szaro said with a mulish expression.

"I don't care. I'm still not kissing that mouth as is," I said with just as stubborn a face.

Szaro emitted a hissing-rattling sound of annoyance, gave me a look as if he was itching to put me across his lap and spank me, then slithered hastily into the house. I felt both hot and bothered by that look, and amused by his aggravation. I went inside to see him in the hygiene room, the dirty dishes sitting on the counter while he thoroughly swished some mouthwash in his mouth. After a good thirty seconds, he spit it out and gave me a 'are you satisfied now?' look.

I chewed my bottom lip, hesitated, then shook my head sheepishly. "Do a second one, just to be on the safe side."

The even louder rattling-hiss that rose from his throat as he complied with undisguised exasperation had me in stitches. I was literally choking with laughter, tears pouring down my face while he glared at me, his cheeks puffing and deflating as he used the mouthwash. Despite his grumpy demeanor, I didn't miss the glimmer of amusement in his eyes, subtle though it was.

Yep, I could definitely see my future Leshu.

When he spit it out, he rinsed his mouth with some water then came to draw me into his embrace. I didn't resist.

"Now, stop denying me, female," he grumbled.

"Kiss away, my dear. You earned it."

And kiss me he did.

With tomorrow being the last day of the First Hunt, the Ordosians and I were venturing deep in the authorized hunting areas to start assessing and mending the damage the rampaging Flayers had caused. It was proving to be an enlightening experience for me. In my five years as a professional Hunter, I'd never really taken the time to evaluate how much the local flora and fauna got wrecked by such incursions, especially when massive, feral beasts ran through areas it normally never did.

Sure, I'd noticed the trampled beds of vegetation and the

trees brought down. But I'd never really thought of the fact that, with a rampage of the scale Trangor experienced, the vegetation crushed underfoot was mostly roots and small berries that constituted the main food source of many small creatures.

I didn't realize that the battles and fallen trees occasionally caused underground collapses of the lairs of burrowing creatures. Some managed to dig their way out, but the squatting species that merely took over abandoned hideouts would become trapped and die of suffocation or starvation.

We found two such families in distress: one was a type of rodent, the other a lizard species. The rodents were extremely weak, but alive. We fed them rugal paste with feeding syringes. It would take them a couple of days to recover, so we left some food in their lair. The lizards didn't fare so well. Both parents had died, the mother still brooding her eggs. We took the eggs and placed them inside one of the incubators on the carrier Drayshan. The caretaker females in the atrium would look after them until they hatched, then they'd be released into the wild again.

The screech of a Flayer in the distance drew our attention. Szaro made me activate my stealth shield and used his own natural camouflage, changing the colors of his scales to make him blend with his surroundings. I hopped onto his back, and he carried me towards the beast. The other hunters, also camouflaged, followed us silently.

Our scanners indicated a Federation hunter was already handling it. I'd found out the Ordosians had regularly been observing us in secret since the beginning of the Hunt. What I hadn't realized was that they'd demanded the Federation remove a couple of hunters from the Hunt because of the cruel methods they used to kill the Flayers. The Ordosians wanted the excess population of these beasts eliminated to maintain a healthy balance, not for them to suffer unnecessarily.

We arrived just in time to witness the battle. My eyes

widened at the sight of the human hunter, Donovan Craigh. We'd developed a healthy friendship over the years of running into each other on the hunting circuits. I'd never seen him in action before. Hunters zealously hid their trade secrets from one another. After all, we were in competition. I almost felt guilty spying on him… almost.

To my surprise, he was using a jetpack to fly around the beast, just out of reach of its long neck. He released four small spheres that hovered around the Flayer's head and emitted a powerful white light, blinding the countless eyes of the creature. The sphere in front of its face broadcast a threatening growling sound. The Flayer immediately snapped its maw of dagger-like teeth while blindly swinging its scythe-like arms. The four spheres flashed their light again to keep it blinded while Donovan quietly hovered behind the creature which was too focused on the growling diversion to realize what was happening.

The clever son of a gun!

He aimed a strange weapon at the legs of the Flayer. A laser tag appeared on the front and back legs on each side of the beast. When he fired, four white balls shot out, each landing on their respective tag. As soon as they made contact, the white substance wrapped around the leg then immediately stretched to connect with the other ball on the same side, trapping the middle legs in the process. The four legs on each side ended up bundled like a bouquet, making the Flayer fall to its stomach. It shouted in outrage, struggling in vain against its restraints.

Donovan flew around to face the creature. He spoke a vocal command, and the spheres each emitted a beam of light at the base of what would be considered the head of the Flayer. It confused me at first, then I realized they were acting as miniature tractor beams, keeping the creature's head immobile while it went on screeching. It allowed Donovan to take perfect aim at the vulnerable spot at the back of its throat. Within seconds, the battle was over.

"Damn," I whispered. "No freaking wonder he's been getting so many perfect scores."

"It is very well done," Szaro whispered back, his voice filled with respect.

"Can I go talk to him for a minute?" I asked. "He's an old friend." I bit back the urge to add that this might be my last chance to ever see him again.

Szaro looked at me over his shoulder then nodded.

"Thank you," I whispered as he let me down.

I kissed his cheek then headed towards Donovan, who was busy claiming his kill with a beacon. I made enough noise so that he would hear my approach. Alerted, his head jerked up as he looked for the source. I deactivated my stealth shield. His shock gave way to disbelief, then to joy.

"Hey girl! What are you doing here? You look well!" he said, rising to his feet.

"I'm doing good. I'm out with the Ordosians, doing ranger stuff. They're hanging out a short way back there." I nodded at the Flayer. "Nice kill. No wonder you've been getting such badass scores."

Donovan snorted. "Says the woman who is so far ahead in the lead, no one has a hope in hell of catching up and winning the grand prize," he said with mocked despair.

I laughed. "Right, but I'm actually not going to claim the grand prize," I said as I came to a stop in front of him. "I already informed the Federation to give it to whoever ends up in second place."

"Why the fuck would you do that? It's five million credits!"

"Because honestly, just the credits I'm making from the kills are way more than I ever hoped for," I said with a shrug. "Plus, it wouldn't be fair. I would never get so many perfect kill bonuses if not for the Ordosians, or that many kills for that matter. You guys are out there doing it on your own. You deserve it more."

"That's really neat of you," Donovan said gently. "But then, you were always a classy lady."

I smiled.

He sobered, concern filling his eyes. "How are you doing, Serena? Everyone was pretty shocked when we heard the news. I can't believe they wanted to execute you for saving one of their own."

I shifted uneasily on my feet. "It's complicated. They didn't want to hurt me, specifically for that reason. But you know what kind of precedent that would have created if I'd just been able to walk away. People would abuse it to try and get away with shit."

He nodded slowly, a frown marring his forehead. "Yeah, I can see that. It still sucks for you though. I mean, we're relieved they found an alternative solution, but are you okay? Are they treating you well?"

"More than well. They're really awesome to me, and I'm loving the life here. Seriously," I insisted when he gave me a dubious look. "You know I've always wanted to become a ranger in a major park. Right now, the entire planet is my playground with the most incredible creatures I've ever seen."

"I can imagine," he conceded. "Their fauna is pretty damn amazing. No wonder the Federation and the UPO are bending over backwards to remain in the Ordosians' good graces. One of the pharma reps gave us a breakdown of all of the medicines and treatments they'll be able to derive from the Flayers alone. It's pretty insane."

"You have no idea," I said with a grin. "Szaro—my husband—was showing me some creature whose empty chrysalis shells can be used to create a cream that regenerates severely burnt skin, among other things."

A troubled expression crossed Donovan's face, immediately putting all of my senses into high alert.

"What is it?" I asked.

Donovan shifted on his feet. "Look, maybe it's nothing, but if you guys are scouting, you might want to head southwest." He hesitated before continuing. "I was there yesterday. With the Flayers becoming more scarce, it was a bit overcrowded with competitors, which is why I decided to come to this sector today. But while I was there, I stumbled on a hunter's bracer."

"A bracer? No arm attached to it?" I asked, taken aback.

"No arm and no blood," Donovan said. "It was pure luck that I found it. I left it with one of my kills for the extraction team to retrieve so they could try to find and rescue its owner. But where I found it didn't feel like it could have fallen there by accident."

"You think its owner deliberately got rid of it so the Federation couldn't track his movements," I said.

Donovan nodded. "When I returned to the base camp last night, everyone was accounted for. I have no clue who it belonged to. But I have my suspicions."

"Oh?"

"With these being the last few days of the Hunt, everyone has been pulling long hours to try and score as many points as possible," he said. "Everyone's score went up noticeably last night, except for three people: Baron, Tholya, and Djomoug."

My heart sank. "Baron, of course," I said through gritted teeth. "Whenever shit goes wrong, he's always involved. But what of the other two? Were there other missing bracers?"

Donovan shook his head. "I only found the one. But it doesn't mean the other two didn't hide theirs better and managed to recover them before going back to the base."

"Where was it stashed?" I asked in a tense voice, a sense of dread washing over me.

"Hang on, let me transfer the coordinates to your map."

Moments later, my bracer beeped with the confirmation. "Thanks. Well, it was really great seeing you again. Give my regards to the others, and take good care of yourself."

"You do the same," he said with a gentle smile.

I nodded in farewell and hastened towards the location where the Ordosians waited for me. Szaro discarded his camouflage long before I reached him.

"I think there might be a problem," I said warily.

"We heard," Szaro said, then gestured at his back with his head. "Get on, my mate."

I complied. While he carried me, piggyback, to where we had left our Drayshans, I wondered about the fact that they'd eavesdropped on our conversation. Well, technically they had not. With their enhanced hearing, they'd been close enough to make out what we were saying without making any effort. I wanted to believe that had simply been the case and not that they had wanted to spy on us from any lack of trust.

When we reached our mounts, one of the hunters took the carrier Drayshan back to the village with the rescued animals and eggs, and the rest of us rode hard to the coordinates Donovan had shared. Szaro had sent a com message to the villages in that vicinity so that they could begin to scout the forbidden sectors nearby for any sign of foul play.

Twenty minutes before we arrived at the coordinates, my chest constricted painfully as the purple light of a distress flare began pulsating overhead. A second and then a third appeared: the Ordosian signal for every off-worlder to leave their forests immediately and retreat into the base camp. Anyone failing to do so would be killed on sight. This was the signal every hunter had feared and that the Federation had dreaded: the confirmation that someone had royally fucked up.

Then the news reached us. A Khenad den had been all but decimated. The creatures were the alien version of a mini-gryphon, with the body of a fennec, a head vaguely resembling that of an owl, and a wide pair of wings. They were among the few creatures on Trangor immune to the Ordosians' appeasing rattling song. Despite their small size, they could do serious damage when feeling threatened. Their vicious talons and their acidic venom could wreck anyone foolish enough to mess with them, especially during birthing season.

By the time we arrived, the hunters of the Cizsa tribe were hard at work tending far too many orphaned hatchlings screaming for food. Tears welled in my eyes at the sight of the countless corpses of the adult Khenads which had only been defending their den.

"I don't understand," I whispered, looking around me. "They all have blaster burns, but no cuts, no organs removed. And all the young are still here. Why this senseless killing?"

"Because of this," Szaro hissed, pointing an angry finger at a series of vine-line branches that ran all over the face of the cave, some of them even crawling inside.

It took me a moment to understand how the vines were relevant to this tragedy. The top section, far out of reach for even the tallest among us, was covered in bright-red flowers with yellow-edged petals that reminded me of marigolds, whereas not a single one could be seen below.

"No!" I whispered, staring at Szaro in disbelief. "They slaughtered these animals to grab some flowers?"

"They're not flowers, but fungus that the Khenads feed on," he ground through his teeth. "Off-worlders call it Attrimat."

I felt the blood drain from my face. Attrimat was a prescription-only, powerful painkiller. In the past couple of years, it had become a highly sought-after recreational drug for the absence of dependency or negative side-effects. As it was extremely difficult to grow, and required specific conditions to do so, its trade was strictly regulated. Judging by the size of the surface that had been plundered, the bastard who had done this would be raking in millions in credits on the black market.

Shortly thereafter, we received news that two more sites had been desecrated. In one, half of the population had been slaughtered, and specific organs removed. The other was a small hidden valley, similar to the one where Szaro and I had made love for the first time. Blind fury washed over me at finding out the son of a bitch had ripped the little Scogas right out of their chrysalis to steal their shells, leaving them to die, half-transformed. In only two or three more days, they would have left the shells on their own.

As soon as the female caretakers of the neighboring villages reached the ravaged sites to take over the care of the surviving creatures, the hunters and I mounted our Drayshans and descended on the Federation base camp.

CHAPTER 16

SZARO

My blood boiled with seething fury. How dared they? And for what? Credits? I never understood the off-worlders' obsession with acquiring riches well-beyond what they required to live comfortably and provide stability and security for their families. But this massacre of innocent creatures out of greed?

Even if they claimed it was to provide therapeutics for their people, nothing justified the senseless killing of one non-threatening species for the exclusive benefit of another. The Flayers had been a global threat that needed to be controlled. The Khenads, the Scogas, and the Varolas had not been a menace to anyone. They'd only wanted to peacefully take care of their young during the birthing season.

In the distance, Federation extraction shuttles were picking up the hunters at various rally points. I wanted them all present when I unleashed my wrath. I tried to silence my unease that Serena would witness me killing one—or more—of her fellow hunters. But she shared my anger. Even now, I could feel the fury tensing her body beneath me and taste it on my tongue as Dagas took us to the off-worlder base.

Like me, she wanted blood.

As Krada had mostly negotiated the Federation's permission to hunt on our planet, and as the village's Great Hunter, it fell to me to render judgement on this atrocity and to exact the punishment I deemed appropriate. A more powerful hunter than I could have laid claim to that role and asked me to step aside, but only my father could have made such a boast. Although the news had undoubtedly reached him by now, Tulma was too far for him to arrive in a timely fashion.

When we cleared the last tree before the Federation base camp, 600 meters ahead, I finally got a good view of just how many hunters from the neighboring villages had joined us. The sound of the hooves of our Drayshans thundered as we surged like a death wave onto the base.

I dismounted before Dagas had come to a full stop then helped Serena down. I removed the lance hanging on my back and held it firmly as I moved forward, Mandha and Raskier flanking me, Serena and the other hunters following behind. The large doors of the base's ship hangar began opening long before we reached them.

A very nervous looking Edocit waited for us at the entrance of the hangar. The vine-like hair of the male appeared withered from stress, as did the flowers that grew on them.

"I am Bron Kflen, the Federation Master Hunter," the male said. "We have received word of the horrible discovery you have made. We—"

"I want the culprits," I hissed, interrupting him.

"We don't know who they are," Bron said in an apologetic, almost pleading tone. "We only have a potential suspect. But we have searched everyone's quarters and shuttles and found nothing."

I pushed past him and entered the hangar where the offworlders were gathered. The room reeked of the fear I could read on every face. To my surprise, none of them were armed. Then again, I could see why the Federation might have ordered it so in order to avoid a regrettable mishap.

Not that it would save them.

"Great Hunter!" Bron exclaimed, chasing after me. "Please, let us resolve this peacefully. The majority of the people here are innocent and respected your rules."

I ignored him, my gaze scanning the room until it landed on the one I'd been seeking. "Zamorian, step forward," I shouted.

The people around him all scattered as if he'd suddenly become infected with a highly transmissible disease.

"I am innocent!" he shouted back, hitting his chest with his four fisted hands. "I am being set up because of the incident with that damn human female!"

"You hid your bracer so that we couldn't track your trespass," I hissed, advancing menacingly by a short distance.

"I didn't hide it! It was stolen from me," the Zamorian argued angrily. "I put on my bracer as usual before going out to hunt. It was only a couple of hours in that I realized it wasn't my real bracer because none of my preset scan configurations worked. I reported it missing then, and the Master Hunter told me it was showing on their radar as being southwest, at least a two-hour ride on speeder from where I was. By the time I got there, it had been recovered by someone else and some extractors brought it back to the base."

"He did contact me about his bracer having been replaced," Bron said cautiously.

"And how do you know that he didn't deliberately use the wrong one to pretend that he was being set up?" I challenged.

"I don't," the Master Hunter conceded. "But I also cannot prove that he did. An accused is innocent until proven guilty. This is all circumstantial."

"Then find me whoever is guilty, or we will consider that you are all conspiring to protect him, and you will equally face our wrath," I snarled.

Outraged shouts answered my statement, many of the people present yelling at the Zamorian to confess.

"You cannot do this!" Bron exclaimed.

"I can and I will."

"Szaro…" the soft voice of my mate called out behind me. My head jerked towards her. She carefully approached and came to a stand next to me. "I have no love for that Zamorian, but Master Bron is right. An accused is innocent until proven guilty. I know more than half of the hunters in this room, and they are upstanding, respectable people who do not deserve to be punished for the crimes of the vermin that did this. Although I don't put it past Baron to have committed those atrocities, we need proof."

"And how do you propose we find this proof, my mate," I said, struggling to keep my anger in check.

"If they found nothing in their quarters or in their personal shuttles, that means that they had a stealth shuttle come retrieve the ill-gotten bounty," she explained. "By the looks of things, the Varolas and the Scogals were slaughtered yesterday. The Khenads were attacked this morning. That means that shuttle is still around. They're either storing everything in its hold, or the shuttle is making regular trips to the space dock to unload the cargo in their acolyte's vessel."

Serena turned to look at the Master Hunter.

"If you haven't already done so, check the ship manifest of the dock for any activity from the ground," my mate said. "Although I suspect you won't find any. If my gut feeling is right, they were too clever for that, and Baron's sorry ass is truly being set up to take the fall."

"Which would mean the shuttle is still down here on Trangor," I said, understanding my female's logic.

"Yes," Serena said with a feral smile. "If we scan for residual energy signatures alongside the border of the forbidden area near those sites, we might be able to track them."

The Master Hunter cast a look at one of the Federation staff and gestured with his head in a way that I assumed meant for him to immediately get on it. I didn't know the technical aspects my mate had referred to, but I understood the general idea. Gratitude and pride filled my heart that she should leverage them to help us achieve justice.

I stiffened, suddenly struck by an idea.

"There's something else you can try," I said to the Master Hunter while glaring at the Zamorian. "The culprit harvested a great deal of Attrimat around the Khenads' den. He would have been covered in spores. Even if he cleaned himself or wore protection, there will likely be traces left on his clothes, speeder, and anything he interacted with."

"Bryna, Tarn, go scan Bayrohnziyiek's room and speeder for spores," Master Bron ordered.

Instead of the panic I had expected, the defiant grin the Zamorian gave me triggered the first spark of doubt in my mind as the two Federation employees left the room. The troubled expression on my mate's face confirmed she, too, had noticed.

"Please have Tholya and Djomoug's rooms and speeders scanned as well," Serena suddenly added.

It took me a moment to identify the two males she had named in the crowd. The shocked and terrified expression etched on their face screamed guilt and panic—the reaction I had expected from the Zamorian. They were a bipedal, furry species that reminded me vaguely of felines.

"Tholya and Djomoug?" Master Bron asked, confused. "Like everyone else, their personal trackers showed them moving all over the forest all day."

"They could have attached their bracers to a preprogrammed drone in camouflage to fool your radars while they traipsed around elsewhere," Serena countered.

"Just like anyone else could have," one of the accused argued.

"Except everyone else made a bunch of kills yesterday," Serena challenged. "But your score and Djomoug's barely moved. How do you explain that?"

"Bad luck!" Djomoug replied in his companion's stead. "The Flayer population has run low now. Everyone is chasing the same ones. We just—"

"Stop arguing," I snapped. "If you have done nothing wrong, then you should have nothing to fear. But if you did, I bet that pretty fur of yours is covered in spores."

"Easy enough to confirm," Master Bron said.

He extended a hand towards one of the Federation staff, who handed him a handheld scanner. He first went to the Zamorian, who spread his four arms wide while staring at me defiantly. Before the Master Hunter even started, whatever suspicions I still held about that male evaporated. He was far too confident to be guilty.

"Clean," the Master Hunter confirmed before turning towards the other two.

They started arguing again, backing away from Master Bron. A human and another Edocit caught the arms of the one called Djomoug, who immediately started struggling to free himself. Master Bron no sooner raised his scanner in front of Djomoug than it went off.

"I invoke the right of sanctuary," Djomoug shouted. "I demand sanctuary! Mercy! Mercy!"

Tholya tried to flee, but Raskier and Mandha—having anticipated it—caught and immobilized him, face down on the floor. Each one had wrapped his tail around one of his legs, and held one of his arms twisted behind his back. I tuned out his pleas for mercy.

"There is no right of sanctuary on Trangor. There is only Ordosian law. And *I* am its enforcer and executioner," I hissed, my fangs descending as I advanced towards Djomoug. "Release him."

The human and Edocit complied, all the other hunters moving further away, forming a circle around us. Djomoug tried to run, but I moved much faster. The minute I caught his arm, Djomoug pivoted on himself, swiping his vicious claws at my face. I bent backward and to the side, my great number of vertebrae allowing me to effortlessly achieve sharp angles without losing my balance. Using my momentum, I spun around, snapping the arm I still held. He cried out in pain and tried to elbow me in the chest. I blocked it with my palm, caught his throat with my other hand and spit acid in his face.

His screeches of pain and the acrid scent of burning flesh only fueled my bloodlust. I pulled the hand he'd covered his melting face with and also snapped that arm at the elbow. I couldn't risk him using his claws on me as he tried to free himself of what would follow. I then backhanded him hard enough that it dislocated his jaw while sending him crashing to the floor. Heedless of Djomoug's gurgling growls of agony, I slithered over him, slowly wrapping the three-meter length of my tail around him.

And then I squeezed.

I felt each of his bones shattering beneath my vise-like grip. The whole time, my gaze never strayed from Tholya, who watched the whole thing with horror. Blood poured out of Djomoug's mouth, nose, and ears moments before he went completely still. I unwrapped my tail from his mangled remains and advanced towards Tholya.

"I don't want to fight you! I won't fight you!" Tholya shouted in a pleading tone.

"You can fight, or you can be executed like the vermin you are," I snarled. "Either way, you die."

"I WON'T FIGHT! YOU CAN'T MAKE ME FIGHT!" he yelled.

"As you wish," I replied.

I looked at my brother then at Raskier. Words were unnecessary. They lifted him by his arms, their tails still keeping his legs shackled. While summoning a ball of venom, I wrapped my hand around his nape and sank my claws into his flesh. As soon as he opened his mouth to scream, I spit the ball to the back of his throat. He nearly choked, cutting his scream short. He instinctively swallowed then coughed, yelping when Raskier and Mandha both dropped him. I turned around and we headed back towards the entrance.

"What… what did you do to me?" Tholya asked in a frightened voice.

The rattling of my tail was his sole response. Within seconds, he was screeching in agony, writhing on the floor as dark veins covered the non-furry parts of his body. Violent spasms shook him, making him brutally smash the back of his head on the hard floor, while foam formed at his mouth. And then he went limp. I stopped rattling my tail—the poison had served its purposes and no longer needed this enhancement.

I allowed the deafening silence to sit in the room for a moment, my gaze roaming over each of the hunters present to make sure they understood worse would happen to any of them who thought to defile our planet like this again. I then turned to their Master Hunter.

"The First Hunt is over," I said in a harsh tone. "You will all be gone by nightfall."

"But you can't—"

"The First Hunt is OVER!" I snapped, baring my fangs at him. "Be gone by nightfall or face the consequences. And find me that shuttle."

I turned towards Serena, bracing for the horror I might find in her gaze. But I found no condemnation in her eyes, only the satisfied glimmer of one who had been vindicated.

My Ashina… My Goddess…

I extended a hand towards her. She took it without hesitation and followed me as I led her out of the hangar, the hunters of the joint tribes shadowing us.

CHAPTER 17
SERENA

Needless to say the shit hit the proverbial fan following the execution of the two Nazhral, Tholya and Djomoug. Their government's demands for reparation only led to them receiving a brutal fine from the United Planets Organization and to all of their hunters being banned from Federation events for the next five years. As the Federation held the most prestigious and lucrative hunts, this was a severe blow to their citizens. These disciplinary measures were brought about after the pilot had confessed their team had been mandated by their officials to acquire the organs and shells. The Attrimat had been Tholya's and Djomoug's personal scheme to enrich themselves.

Following my suggestion, they'd been able to track down the signature of the shuttle that had been used. After the flares had gone up, the shuttle had made a hasty return to the space dock, and its pilot had attempted to flee aboard the Nazhral ship with all of their loot. But Master Hunter Bron thankfully had the foresight of forbidding any departures from the space dock until everything was sorted out. The pilot and his bounty were handed over to the Cizsa tribe. I didn't even want to imagine what fate befell him. But at least, the Attrimat they recovered would provide for the orphaned Khenads. Of the adults, only a couple of females and a male had survived. They were grievously injured, but with the cream from the Scogas' shells, the caretakers hoped they would recover enough to be functional mentors to the countless young in need of guidance.

To my relief, Szaro's edict that the Federation leave at once had not been a permanent rupture of any association. Despite his fury, my husband had actually made them leave for their own safety. Judging by the extent of the anger that had spread through the tribes as the news reached them, things might have turned ugly had any Ordosian run into an off-worlder. Once everyone cooled off, they would recognize that out of the hundred or so hunters that came to Trangor, only two truly violated their laws—in a most abject way—and one flirted with disaster.

It warmed my heart when Kayog Voln reached out to me, not to ask me to intervene in favor of the UPO or the Federation, but to thank me for tempering things when Szaro had seemed to want to go on a bloody rampage, and to ask if I was faring well.

Trades with the UPO would continue, but any future hunts would need to be thoroughly discussed.

However, these days, the Federation was the least of my concerns. I had a front row seat to the spectacle of the Ordosian version of a man flu. Szaro was beginning to molt. His miserable face would put even the most shameless puppy to shame. Not a single wall in the house had been spared from him scratching against it. Hydrating a lot helped the old skin detach, so Szaro was downing gallons upon gallons of water, which meant he also constantly needed to pee. During that time, he developed a new appreciation for an in-house hygiene room, especially since, in his infinite wisdom, Irco had also included a waste chute for Szaro next to my toilet.

When the itching became too much for him to handle, we soaked in the crazy Jacuzzi tub Irco had also built next to the separate shower. Elevated on a dais, it gave us a stunning view of the hidden valley outside. As I cuddled with Szaro and scraped his scales with a scrubbing stone, he made the sexiest rattling-purrs that totally messed with my girly bits.

One week into it, he awoke to find the old skin of his left arm falling off. I nearly peed myself laughing as he did an excessively happy dance. That evening, the one from the right arm also went bye-bye. As much as I enjoyed teasing him, I sympathized with his situation. It genuinely looked uncomfortable. But his new scales underneath were absolutely gorgeous. I couldn't believe I used to think his old ones gleamed. In comparison, they looked dull and faded.

Today was our day off. Although the Ordosians followed a seven-day week calendar, there were no official days off such as weekends. You took a day off when you wanted. Generally, people worked three to four days in a row then took one or two days to rest. Most of it was coordinated with others to make sure there was always someone to cover the needs in their respective field. Szaro spent the morning with Mandha while I went swimming with Salha, little Eicu, and the other females and children of the village.

A few of them gave me strange looks that I couldn't interpret. When I asked Salha about it, she simply said that I smelled good, that I smelled healthy. How could I not while living the healthiest life ever here on Trangor?

Szaro was already home when I returned.

"Ready for our trip down the valley!" I said happily as I strutted my way towards him.

His welcoming grin stiffened and a nearly savage expression stole across his features, stopping me dead in my tracks. He flicked his tongue a couple of times my way, and a deep, drawn-out, rattling-growl rose from his throat as he menacingly slithered towards me.

"Szaro?" I said warily, unsure if I was turned on or scared.

"You are ripe," he said through gritted teeth.

"What?"

"You're in heat…" he said, drawing me into his embrace before crushing my lips in a passionate kiss.

Right… I would be ovulating right now. No wonder the females thought I smelled good… *healthy*. Szaro and I hadn't discussed children. Honestly, I hadn't felt there was any point to it, first because this wasn't something we should even consider until we were certain I would stay here, and second because I genuinely didn't think we were compatible that way. Either way, I had a contraceptive implant in case we turned out to be more compatible than I thought. Still, I now felt that we would need to openly discuss the matter, if only for him to be aware that no pregnancies were possible at the moment so that he wouldn't feel blindsided.

But Szaro's feverish hands all but ripping the clothes off my back kicked those serious thoughts to the curb and brought me back to the here and now. I lifted my arms to let him rid me of my top. As soon as it was gone, he pushed me against the wall of the hallway. His mouth dove for one of my breasts, and his hands started stripping me of my skirt. Szaro loooooved skirts, which he found highly convenient to get quick access to my naughty bits without having to undress me.

He never gave me a chance to step out of my skirt. As soon as I lifted a leg to do so, he lowered himself in front of me, slipped that leg over his shoulder, and buried his face between my thighs. I moaned and rubbed the scales of his hood while he devoured me. Szaro had become quite the expert at going down on me, his crazy tongue flicking inside me just the right way to drive me insane, while his fingers quickly brought me to the edge.

I was seconds from toppling over when Szaro suddenly pulled away from me with an enraged growl. I slipped and landed on my ass with a yelp. Stunned and disoriented, I stared in disbelief as Szaro slammed his back on the opposite wall, rocking from side to side as he scratched. Too many emotions, from shock to disbelief, coursed through me in quick succession. But the blissful expression on his face as he frantically scratched did me in. I burst out laughing, the dull throbbing in my right butt cheek where I'd landed soon forgotten.

When the itching subsided, Szaro's saw me still sitting on the floor. His mortified expression had me hiccupping with choked laughter. He picked me up and carried me to the bedroom. But I didn't let him put me on the bed. Instead, I ordered him to lie down on the floor so that he could scratch his back on its rough surface should he once again get an urgent itch to alleviate.

Even though I'd been cheated out of my orgasm, I didn't mind. Szaro's magic cock would have me singing arias in no time. He'd not been kidding when he'd said that once I'd been with an Ordosian, I'd have no time for human men. My husband had ruined me for any other male. The things he did with his cock were indescribable. Just thinking of how he made his spikes massage my inner walls, hitting my G-spot just the right way over and over again, had me aching to be filled. To think a spiked peen had terrified me. How clueless I had been… And I also loved going down on my man and seeing him fall apart for me. It didn't hurt that his self-lubricant tasted vaguely like honey.

But right now, I was too impatient to finish what he'd started, especially since I didn't know how long we had before another bout of itching had him bucking me off. As soon as he was lying on his back, I straddled him and clawed at his scales around his pelvis to make him extrude. He did so without hesitation, and hissed with pleasure when I wrapped my hand around his length to give it a few strokes before impaling myself on it.

Good heavens! I would never get enough of this. It wasn't just the insanely blissful feel of him inside of me, but the way he looked at me that touched me every time we made love. Szaro was definitely falling in love with me. And I couldn't deny that I was falling hard for him. I'd always considered myself rather vanilla when it came to sex, but with him, I liked exploring different positions. Szaro loved it because he never could have done that had he ended up with an Ordosian female.

But as was his wont, he soon took control of our coupling, even if I was the one riding him. Slipping his hands under my bum, he effortlessly lifted me up as if I weighed nothing and started pumping up into me. I pressed my palms to his muscular chest for support and threw my head back with a strangled moan as his magical cock set me on fire. Each thrust, each stroke had my eyes nearly rolling to the back of my head.

My orgasm slammed into me out of the blue. I cried out and collapsed, boneless on top of him. Without slowing down, Szaro wrapped one arm around me, holding me tightly against him, and fisted the hair at my nape with the other before claiming my mouth in a demanding kiss. Our tongues mingled while he pounded into me from below, a second climax building as the first one waned.

When I cried out in bliss again, Szaro joined his voice to mine as his seed shot into me. He whispered my name in an almost pained voice followed by a series of words in Ordosian that I didn't understand. And yet, they messed me up. In my heart, I knew he'd told me he loved me. But he wasn't done yet. Twice more he made me climax, one of them with the enhanced effect of his aphrodisiac rattle. Each time, he filled me with his seed. On the final one, as soon as he'd shot out the last drop, the head of his cock began swelling inside of me.

Szaro often did that while making love to me. Aside from his control over the spikes covering it, my man could expand the tip of his cock for greater friction. He normally did that while pulling out, which gave my sensitive spot an extra jolt, but narrowed it on his way back in.

But this was different.

His head expanded not to the point of being painful, but

enough that he couldn't pull out. We were effectively locked together. I knew canines and lupine species often knotted with their mates, but I'd never heard of this with a reptilian species.

With my head resting on his chest, listening as his heartbeat slowed to a normal tempo, I pondered how to address the issue, or if now was even the right time. His big hand lazily caressing my back made it hard to concentrate.

Taking a deep breath, I lifted my head to look him straight in the eye. The languid expression on his face faded when he saw the one on mine. His features took on that attentive air he always had whenever we were discussing a serious matter.

"You knotted with me," I said in a soft, factual voice.

"It is not a knot," Szaro corrected gently. "But yes, we are locked."

"Why?" I asked.

Szaro studied my features for a few moments as if searching for a clue as to where my head was at before answering. "You know why," he said in a conversational tone. "It increases the chances of conception. You are fertile."

I licked my lips nervously, kicking myself for delaying this conversation. I should have done it right after the first time we'd made love.

"We have not discussed having offspring," I said carefully.

"We have not," he conceded.

"In truth, that's not a conversation I expected us to have at all, or at least not before I'd made a decision as to whether or not I would stay on Trangor after the six months agreed upon," I said, feeling guilty for even speaking those words. But we needed to lay it all on the table.

"We have coupled many, many times for nearly a month now," Szaro argued. "For all we know, my seed may have already taken root. You may already be carrying my offspring. Would it be so terrible?"

The wistfulness in his voice as he spoke those words broke

my heart. Another wave of guilt twisted my innards as I searched for the kindest words to shatter his illusions. It was all the more distressing to have this conversation while locked in such an intimate fashion with him.

"No, it wouldn't be terrible," I conceded. "You are a wonderful male. But a child is a lifetime commitment. I would want to make sure that the father of my children will be the male I will spend the rest of my life with."

He nodded slowly, an unreadable expression on his face. "But you're still unsure if you want that male to be me," he said factually.

"Actually, I do want that male to be you," I said, surprised by my own words, but nonetheless struck by their veracity. "I just need to be sure that you are. Humans normally court for many months, sometimes even years before making a life commitment. This is too soon for me to make such a decision. But I really, really like you. Even though it can be challenging at times with our cultural and anatomical differences, I love living on Trangor."

His face melted into a tender expression that turned me upside down. "Then why worry so much, my mate? If I make you happy and you find joy in your life here, then all else will fall into place as it is meant to be," Szaro said, caressing my cheek with his knuckles. "I am already committed for life where you are concerned. An offspring would only be the embodiment of my feelings for you, and of our bond. You are where you were always meant to be. But as you wish for more time, I will honor your request. If you haven't already conceived—"

"I haven't conceived," I interrupted gently, guilt rearing its head again. "I can't conceive right now." Szaro frowned, a confused expression on his face. "I mean, first off, I don't even know that you and I are compatible that way. Our species are very different. I don't think a human and an Ordosian can have offspring together. But even if we can, there's no way I can be pregnant right now. Long before I even came to Trangor, I got a contraceptive implant. It's still good for two years. As long as it's inside my arm, I won't be able to conceive. My plan was to remove it after our six months, if I decided to stay here."

"I see," Szaro said, failing miserably to hide his disappointment.

"I'm sorry," I said, feeling horrible. "I—"

"Do not apologize, my mate," Szaro said in a reassuring tone. "I won't deny that I am saddened to hear this. I dream of seeing you swell with my offspring. You may not have chosen me yet, but I have definitely chosen you. I want none other than you. Still, you acted wisely. I am the one at fault for not discussing it with you. It would destroy me if we did have a young, and you decided to leave me, and I lost you both."

"Let's just agree that *we* should both have brought it up the minute we started playing naughty," I said, relieved. This had gone down much better than I'd expected.

"Agreed," Szaro said softly. "Thank you for your honesty. You could have kept it secret, and I would have merely assumed that we weren't compatible or had failed to conceive."

"I don't want lies between us," I said with a frown. "Whatever this is, and wherever it's going, it will be based on honesty."

Szaro grinned and tightened his embrace around me. "Then let me give you this piece of honesty," he said with a tender smile. "I will continue to lock with you whenever you are in your fertile period, even if it is pointless. I love being this closely joined with you. I also do not worry about your uncertainties. You are my soulmate. The Goddess plucked you from the stars and sent you to me. You were made for me and for this world. In your heart, I believe you already know it. But take the human time you need. Nothing will change the inevitable."

CHAPTER 18

SERENA

Things changed after that conversation… in a positive way. Or rather, I changed. Szaro continued to be his loving, caring, and supportive self. I just dropped any walls I still kept erected between us.

While we lay together, locked on the floor, I did a lot of introspection and soul-searching. I realized just how much I'd been keeping him at arm's length. Sure, I went hunting with them, shared his bed, and played house with him, but I never really immersed myself in the Ordosian life nor fully opened myself to him or truly let him in.

It had been a self-defense mechanism to leave me a way out. He was too easy to fall in love with, and the thought of uprooting myself to permanently settle on a planet deemed primitive in many respects was terrifying. But it was the fear of change, of the unknown that had been holding me back. In the end, the true question was whether I was happy here, and the answer was a resounding yes. But more importantly, I didn't think a world or a male existed who could make me happier than I had been here so far.

That acknowledgement lifted a huge weight off my shoulders. Szaro was right, in my heart, I already knew that I would stay here with him. I just needed my 'human time' to be sure I wasn't rushing in.

Conveying this news to my parents didn't go as smoothly. Because of the great distance and the basic technology of the Ordosians, a special relay had to be temporarily set up to allow direct communication. A couple of days after the pregnancy talk with Szaro, I had my usual monthly call with my parents. Naturally, they'd been informed of my situation, and had tried—and failed—to leverage all of their contacts in high places to get me out of Trangor.

Five days later, Szaro's old skin fell off—in one single piece—at long last. It was quite impressive. The look on his face was priceless. You'd think he was having an orgasm right there and then. He looked bigger, taller, and definitely more stunning as he strutted about in his shiny new skin. But the shadow of my parents' disapproval dampened the pleasure of witnessing my husband's relief.

In the following weeks, I received a barrage of messages from my parents raising the million reasons why it didn't make sense for me to stay here and all the dangers that involved. I easily countered the majority of their arguments, demonstrating that the same would be true pretty much anywhere else I decided to settle that wasn't a human colony. That said, one of their arguments did concern me.

In the second week of my arrival on Trangor, I'd received the medical pod I'd ordered. To my shock and delight, the UPO—at the request of Kayog—had it upgraded free of charge to the most advanced model available on the market. Shaped like a stasis chamber, the machine allowed me to self-diagnose, suggested and applied treatments, and could perform some fairly advanced surgeries. It could even assist with child delivery. Worst case scenario, if I ended up in a critical state where it couldn't treat me, the pod would put me in stasis and send a distress signal to my designated emergency contact so that they could come and assist me.

That, and the fact that the Ordosian healer, Teichi, had begun learning human anatomy and physiology so she could look after me should the need arise, had given me a great deal of peace of mind. But that was short-lived.

Just a few days shy of my third month on Trangor, I developed rashes along my spine and arms. I had a slight but persistent fever, frequent stomach cramps, and nausea, especially triggered by specific smells. The medical pod failed to identify the cause. I wasn't pregnant. I wasn't having an allergic reaction. I wasn't poisoned or infected by any sort of virus or bacteria. And yet, the pod kept giving me the conflicting message that my body was under attack but failed to identify the cause or eliminate the "foreign" entity attacking it.

Szaro was beside himself with worry. We contacted Kayog to arrange for me to be seen by one of the traveling human doctors of the UPO. As it would require me to leave the planet for a couple of days—in direct breach of the agreement that had initially spared me from execution—it needed to be handled carefully. I doubted the Elders, or any of the other tribes, would have challenged my temporary departure under the circumstances and in light of the strong bonds I had developed with them over the past three months. But to have Szaro say he would defy the Elders and any opposition, even if that meant his banishment, to see me treated, moved me to the core.

I'd fallen hard for my Ordosian. And every day since had only confirmed what he had known all along: I'd been created for him, and he for me.

But that discussion with the Elders became a non-issue. As the trade agreements with the pharmaceutical industries of the UPO had been maintained, they sent a team every two weeks to collect what the Ordosians had saved or gathered for them. Since a pickup was scheduled on the day after tomorrow, Kayog offered to have a medical expert come to Trangor instead. The Federation base camp—which in fact belonged to the UPO—possessed a top-of-the-line medical bay in case one of the hunters or other UPO representatives got severely injured by the vicious local fauna.

We jumped on that opportunity. Szaro had trusted me to return after being treated if we had gone the first route. But he had hated the thought of not being by my side, especially since we didn't know how long the doctors might decide to keep me once they—hopefully—figured out what was wrong with me.

Although I'd regained the use of my speeder to travel around Trangor, I shared a ride with Szaro on Dagas as I didn't feel steady enough to control my vehicle. To my delight, we were greeted by a woman, Dr. Ahmad. I'd always felt more comfortable with female practitioners. And, in this instance, as she would strip me naked, poke and prod me in every way possible in the presence of Szaro, it certainly eliminated a great deal of potential awkwardness.

And she certainly did test the fuck out of me.

I had blood and samples of every possible type drawn from me. I was still mortified by some of the *very* personal questions I had to answer, from my diet and hygiene, to my medical history and detailed sex life.

Yes, dear doctor, I have gone down many times on my husband's alien dick and swallowed. It tastes like honey with a dab of salt. Anything else you'd like to know?

Groan…

The delay in getting tangible results or even the slightest hint as to the cause of my condition was seriously starting to freak me out. When she asked to run some tests on Szaro, I nearly panicked. What the fuck was going on? Despite his obvious worry, Szaro submitted willingly. He would do whatever was needed to see me get better.

After at least four hours of this circus, the doctor met with us to go over her findings. I sat in a chair across the table from her, and Szaro settled next to me, sitting in that funky way on his tail and holding my hand.

"So, the good news is that you are not ill," Dr. Ahmad said carefully. "You do not have a disease that needs to be treated."

I heaved a sigh of relief. "So, it's an allergic reaction?" I asked.

The doctor hesitated. "You could put it that way. The problem is your contraceptive implant. Your body is reacting to —rejecting really—the progestogen that it is steadily releasing into your bloodstream."

I recoiled and stared at her in confusion. "What? That doesn't make sense," I argued. "I've been using this implant for years without any problem."

"Right," the doctor conceded. "But that was *before.*"

"What do you mean? Why do you say 'before' like that?" I asked.

The doctor studied my face, while chewing her bottom lip, clearly trying to find the right words to drop the bombshell I knew was incoming. She cast a glance at Szaro, who was staring intently at her, then seemed to make a decision.

"What you assumed to be rashes on your body are in fact mutations," Dr. Ahmad said.

"WHAT?!" I exclaimed.

"What kind of mutations?" Szaro hissed.

"Relax, both of you," Dr. Ahmad said in a soft voice, raising her palms in an appeasing gesture. "It is nothing bad. You're not turning into some kind of monster. You're adapting."

"Adapting to what?" I asked, on the verge of panic.

"To your husband."

I froze, my brain tilting for a moment. Then I turned to Szaro, who stared at me with the same stunned expression.

"We know very little about Ordosians, which is why I ran some tests on Mr. Kota," Dr. Ahmad explained. "Initially, I thought you were having an allergic or toxic reaction to mating with your husband. While coupling between you is obviously possible, the Ordosian and human reproductive systems are not compatible. Sure enough, all of your tests showed a large presence of alien DNA and hormones in your system."

"I'm hurting my mate?" Szaro asked with such pain in his voice and such a crestfallen expression that it broke my heart.

"No, Mr. Kota. Not exactly," Dr. Ahmad said in a gentle voice. "Contrary to what I assumed, your DNA and hormones aren't acting like a foreign element, or virus or bacteria. They have have become an inherent part of you, Mrs. Bello. The lining of your uterus has changed—or rather it is changing. Your entire endocrine system is also changing. Your body is adapting so that you can bear an Ordosian child. And your contraceptive implant is messing with that."

My free hand flew to my stomach as I gaped at the doctor. From the start, I'd known in my gut that Szaro and I were too different to have children, but this changed everything. I turned to look at Szaro, who was staring at my stomach with an air of wonder and longing. My throat constricted. He looked up and our gazes locked. Words weren't necessary. His eyes told me everything about his hopes and dreams for us.

Tearing my eyes away from him, I forced myself to turn back to the doctor.

"And what about the redness?" I asked. "You said they're not rashes."

The doctor cleared her throat and shifted in her chair, looking at me sheepishly. "You should develop some scales there."

"I'm going to be covered in scales?!"

"NO! No, no. Not at all. Or rather, there's really no reason to think so," Dr. Ahmad amended. "These changes are purely cosmetic and should be constrained to the spots where you currently have the redness that you assumed to be rashes. So, around your nape and down your spine, and on the outer side from the curve of your shoulders to your forearm. If they bother you, I believe they could be surgically removed, but I can't guarantee they wouldn't come back."

"Wow, okay," I said, feeling overwhelmed.

"Can this be reversed?" Szaro asked.

I felt gut-punched upon hearing those words. I turned to look at him disbelievingly. Why the fuck would he ask something like that? Had he changed his mind? Now that this had become a reality, was he reconsidering wanting children with me?

"Yes, it can be," Dr. Ahmad said carefully. "It's borderline, but there is still time… as long as we begin treatment immediately or in the next couple of days. However, that would mean no more fluid exchange between the two of you, mainly of semen and hormone, whether through penetration or orally. So, you could remain active, but use condoms. Mrs. Bello would also need to undergo hormonal treatment."

I felt faint.

"Thank you, Dr. Ahmad," I said, still staring at Szaro, who was holding my gaze unwaveringly. "Can you give us a moment, please?"

"Yes, of course," the doctor replied.

She jumped to her feet and exited the room as if she couldn't get out fast enough. I dropped whatever pretense of control I still possessed and let my face show how hurt I felt right now.

"Why would you ask that? You no longer want children with me?" I asked.

"I love you, Serena Bello," Szaro said forcefully. "I want to spend the rest of my life with you, with a swarm of offspring filling our dwelling. I want to carve every centimeter of our home's entrance with the decades of memories we will forge together. I want to fill the walls of our younglings' rest rooms with their history as they grow and thrive. I want to travel every corner of Trangor with you by my side, show you the beauty of this world and rediscover it through your eyes. And I want us to have all of this because you *choose* me, because you *choose* us and that future. Not because you are trapped by a biological and hormonal reaction."

My chest constricted, and a wave of love washed over me.

"Do you want me to reverse this?" I asked, my eyes flicking between his.

"I want you to do what feels right for yourself," he said firmly. "Whatever choice you make, I will support you. Your decision must not be made because you feel pressured by some arbitrary deadline or feel like your body is taking that decision away from you."

"And what if I said I didn't want to reverse it?"

A powerful emotion crossed Szaro's face. He swallowed painfully, and his hand tightened around mine.

"I would ask you why not," he whispered.

"What if I said it was because I, too, want to see you cover our dwelling's entrance with even more carvings than your father has done for Erastra?" I asked, my eyes prickling from overwhelming emotions.

"I would respond that this makes me the happiest male in the universe," he said, pulling me out of my chair to make me straddle him.

"What if I said it was because I've fallen madly in love with you, and I can't picture myself with anyone else, since you've ruined me for any other male?" I asked, wrapping my arms around his neck and pressing my forehead against his.

"I'd say I told you so," he replied before capturing my lips in a passionate kiss.

EPILOGUE
SZARO

My mate had Dr. Ahmad remove her implant the same day. We agreed with the doctor that regular follow ups would be wise as this was the first coupling between an Ordosian and a human on record. The doctor promised to come for an in-person visit once every other month, but Serena would send her bi-weekly self-diagnostics she performed with the medical pod, which had been reconfigured to account for our unique situation.

Within 48 hours of removing the implant, all the negative symptoms my mate had displayed vanished. Two weeks later, beautiful golden scales, even more gorgeous than I had imagined, graced my female's arms and the line of her spine. A few scattered ones adorned her pelvic area. They glimmered under the sun, making her look even more like the *Ashina* she was to me. I'd insisted she wear sleeveless clothes and backless dresses as often as possible for all to see the stunning manifestation of our bond. To her delight, my mate also gained a noticeable increase in physical strength and more acute hearing.

Things didn't go too well when Serena first communicated those changes to her parents and her decision to permanently stay on Trangor. A few months went by without them so much as responding to her calls or messages. But eventually, they rebuilt those bridges. They were family.

Although Serena learned how to ride a Drayshan on her own, she mainly stuck to sharing Dagas with me, which I certainly didn't mind. She also fully integrated with our culture and helped expand it. While most of her time was dedicated to the hunter's work of scouting and caring for the wilderness alongside me, she spent quite a bit of time with Salha learning the caretakers' role. And Elder Krathi took great pleasure in teaching her the lore and history of the Ordosian people.

But the biggest immersion came from touring the countless tribes of Trangor. After our return from Tulma, word of Serena's dancing prowess had traveled quickly. Naturally, our own tribe had demanded a live performance. Serena had done a different dance than the one at our second bonding, but just as spectacular. While Ordosians weren't a highly social people, our artistically inclined tribe members performed once every ten to twelve days on the circle. Serena officially became part of that rotation. Not only did she mesmerize us with the ribbons, she also did incredible things with a ball and with oddly-shaped sticks that she called clubs.

At first, a number of hunters from other tribes came to Krada to get a peek. But as most Ordosian females did not travel away from their village, many clamored for Serena to come to them. It would be easier anyway to allow everyone to witness firsthand her incredible talent. So, travel we did, matching those performances with the long-range scouting schedule we had already planned.

The six-month deadline came and went. Although I'd already known that Serena was fully committed to our relationship, I still breathed a lot easier when it was officially over. The following month, we authorized another Federation Hunt, this time, for a far more lethal and insidious creature than the Flayers. With an even stricter selection process, the Federation hoped—and succeeded—in avoiding any regrettable incidents this time around.

On the last day of the Hunt, Serena announced she was pregnant.

Even now, I fail to understand how the walls didn't collapse, I shouted so loudly with joy. Needless to say, I drove my mate insane from being overly protective. My mother came to stay with us to look after my female and her soon-to-be second grandchild. This both helped and made matters worse. For all that, Serena was grateful for the support. She was stressing far more than she would admit at the thought that something could go wrong with the first human-Ordosian offspring.

To my delight, she voluntarily stepped back from any scouting runs, even at the very beginning of her pregnancy when Dr. Ahmad said it would technically be safe. Instead, my mate dove into a project she'd been toying with for a while. She began to write a detailed encyclopedia of the flora and fauna of Trangor. Beyond facts and images, she included lore and folklore related to them, stories which she had gathered from the Elders of each village we'd visited. While it had been intended for offworlders, it also became an educational reference for our own people.

To Serena's dismay, she experienced her first contractions around noon, exactly six months and eight days after she announced her pregnancy. Thirty-four minutes later, we welcomed our little Sethe into the world. As Ordosian pregnancies normally lasted five months, when Serena's neared the six-month mark, we assumed it would take the full nine-months humans did. Considering the speed at which she went from the start of labor to the little one coming out, she'd feared he was premature or in distress.

But our son was beyond perfect.

I stood transfixed as I gazed upon him. I had never seen an Ordosian with black scales. His shone like obsidian. Silver scales covered the rim of his hood while a smattering of them adorned his shoulders. By its size and thickness, his long tail marked him as a hunter and hinted that he would grow as massive, if not more, as my father. Sethe looked at his mother with silver eyes, the slit-shaped pupils a little wider than usual for an Ordosian. He smiled, his tiny fangs poking out.

"He is magnificent, my mate," I said, my throat constricted with emotion.

"He is," she said with a nod, tears brimming in her eyes. "He's his father's spitting image." She turned to look at me with a world of love in her eyes. "The day Kayog told me I had to marry an Ordosian to avoid execution, I thought my life was over. I never would have imagined it was in fact the beginning of a fairy tale. Thank you for saving my life and for committing to me when I was too blind to see that my happiness was standing right before me."

"Thank you for giving us a chance and for giving me the family I always dreamt of but didn't think possible," I replied, caressing her cheek with my knuckles. "I love you, Serena."

"I love you, too, Szaro."

THE END

S GRIFFIN

SZARO & SERENA

SZARO & SERENA

SCOGA

FLAYER

ALSO BY REGINE ABEL

THE VEREDIAN CHRONICLES

Escaping Fate

Blind Fate

Raising Amalia

Twist of Fate

Hands of Fate

Defying Fate

BRAXIANS

Anton's Grace

Ravik's Mercy

Krygor's Hope

XIAN WARRIORS

Doom

Legion

Raven

Bane

Chaos

Varnog

Reaper

Wrath

Xenon

VALOS OF SONHADRA

Unfrozen

Iced

BLOOD MAIDENS OF KARTHIA

Claiming Thalia

PRIME MATING AGENCY

I Married A Lizardman

I Married A Naga

I Married A Birdman

I Married A Merman

THE MIST

The Mistwalker

The Nightmare

EMPATHS OF LYRIA

An Alien For Christmas

THE SHADOW REALMS

Dark Swan

OTHER

True As Steel

Bluebeard's Curse

Alien Awakening

Heart of Stone

The Hunchback

ABOUT REGINE

USA Today bestselling author Regine Abel is a fantasy, paranormal and sci-fi junky. Anything with a bit of magic, a touch of the unusual, and a lot of romance will have her jumping for joy. She loves creating hot alien warriors and no-nonsense, kick-ass heroines that evolve in fantastic new worlds while embarking on action-packed adventures filled with mystery and the twists you never saw coming.

Before devoting herself as a full-time writer, Regine had surrendered to her other passions: music and video games! After a decade working as a Sound Engineer in movie dubbing and live concerts, Regine became a professional Game Designer and Creative Director, a career that has led her from her home in Canada to the US and various countries in Europe and Asia.

Facebook

https://www.facebook.com/regine.abel.author/

Website

https://regineabel.com

Regine's Rebels Reader Group

https://www.facebook.com/groups/ReginesRebels/

Newsletter

http://smarturl.it/RA_Newsletter

Goodreads

http://smarturl.it/RA_Goodreads

Bookbub

https://www.bookbub.com/profile/regine-abel

Amazon

http://smarturl.it/AuthorAMS

CPSIA information can be obtained
at www.ICGtesting.com
Printed in the USA
LVHW020214080222
710478LV00015B/2082

9 781989 761977